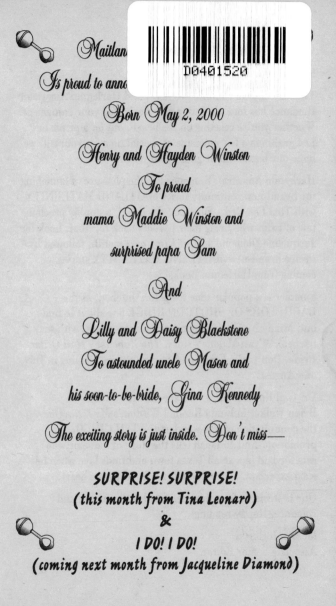

Maitland

Is proud to announce

Born May 2, 2000

Henry and Hayden Winston

To proud

mama Maddie Winston and

surprised papa Sam

And

Lilly and Daisy Blackstone

To astounded uncle Mason and

his soon-to-be-bride, Gina Kennedy

The exciting story is just inside. Don't miss—

SURPRISE! SURPRISE!
(this month from Tina Leonard)
&
I DO! I DO!
(coming next month from Jacqueline Diamond)

Dear Reader,

The lazy days of summer are here, and Harlequin American Romance has four charming new stories for your enjoyment! Whether you're relaxing on the beach, out on a picnic or just grabbing a few moments of special time for yourself, we hope our books will brighten your days.

Harlequin American Romance has the pleasure of launching the brand-new continuity series MAITLAND MATERNITY with Tina Leonard's *Surprise! Surprise!*, a doubly precious tale of twins who bring their parents back together. Look for Jacqueline Diamond's *I Do! I Do!* next month, followed by *twelve* brand-new MAITLAND MATERNITY stories, coming from Harlequin Books!

Summer is a popular time for gettin' hitched, as the BACHELORS OF SHOTGUN RIDGE are about to find out! Mindy Neff's exciting new miniseries begins with sexy bachelor Wyatt Malone's story, *The Rancher's Mail-Order Bride*. Don't miss Ethan and Stony's stories, coming in July and August!

Dr. Gail Roberts has a very special little gift for Brian Walker in Linda Randall Wisdom's *My Little One*, the continuation of our wonderful WITH CHILD... promotion. And Jo Leigh tells the story of a doctor who gets waylaid in a small Texas town and finds love when he least expects it. *Doctor, Darling* will steal your heart!

Our best wishes for a summer filled with warmth and romance. Happy reading!

Melissa Jeglinski
Associate Senior Editor

Surprise! Surprise!

TINA LEONARD

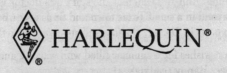

HARLEQUIN®

TORONTO • NEW YORK • LONDON
AMSTERDAM • PARIS • SYDNEY • HAMBURG
STOCKHOLM • ATHENS • TOKYO • MILAN • MADRID
PRAGUE • WARSAW • BUDAPEST • AUCKLAND

Special thanks and acknowledgment are given to
Tina Leonard for her contribution to the
Maitland Maternity series.

To Isabel Sites, Georgina Haynes, Leesa Whitson,
Olivia Holton, Suzanne Coleburn and Ken Lester,
Donita Lawrence, Oleta North, Denise O'Sullivan and
Natashya Wilson. Without all of the above-mentioned people,
the author Tina Leonard might not exist.

ISBN 0-373-16829-2

SURPRISE! SURPRISE!

Visit us at www.eHarlequin.com

Printed in U.S.A.

ABOUT THE AUTHOR

Tina Leonard loves to laugh, which is one of the many reasons she loves writing Harlequin American Romance books. In another lifetime, Tina thought she would be single and an East Coast fashion buyer forever. The unexpected happened when Tina met Tim again after many years—she hadn't seen him since they'd attended school together from first through eighth grade. They married, and now Tina keeps a close eye on her school-age children's friends! Lisa and Dean keep their mother busy with soccer, gymnastics and horseback riding. They are proud of their mom's "kissy books" and eagerly help her any way they can. Tina hopes that readers will enjoy the love of family she writes about in her books. Recently a reviewer wrote, "Leonard has a wonderful sense of the ridiculous," which Tina loved so much, she wants it for her epitaph. Right now, however, she's focusing on her wonderful life and writing a lot more romance!

Books by Tina Leonard

HARLEQUIN AMERICAN ROMANCE

Don't miss any of our special offers. Write to us at the following address for information on our newest releases.

Harlequin Reader Service
U.S.: 3010 Walden Ave., P.O. Box 1325, Buffalo, NY 14269
Canadian: P.O. Box 609, Fort Erie, Ont. L2A 5X3

CAST OF CHARACTERS

Sam Winston—Went from making business deals to changing babies' diapers.

Maddie Winston—Got tired of waiting for motherhood!

Henry and Hayden Winston—Twin baby brothers born by a miracle of love.

Virgil and Franny Brady & Severn and Sara Winston—They'd try anything to get their children back together again, especially baby-sit.

Joey Brady—Maddie's younger brother's near miss turns out to be a blessing in disguise.

Dr. Abby Maitland—She's delivered hundreds of babies, but twins are her favorites.

Dr. Mitchell Maitland—He's helped dozens of couples have the families they've always wanted.

Megan Maitland—The founder of Maitland Maternity has a special place in her heart for all the children born here.

Mason and Gina Blackstone—Read about their story in *I Do! I Do!* coming next month.

Daisy and Lilly Blackstone—Twin baby sisters born prematurely who bring together a lonely rancher and a virginal nurse, in *I Do! I Do!*

Chapter One

"Without Maitland Maternity, and Dr. Mitchell Maitland, this miracle wouldn't have happened." Maddie Winston swallowed, her eyes glowing with soft happiness as she looked at her precious newborns. Twin boys. She still couldn't believe it. A grateful sigh tightened her throat but she looked at the newspaper reporters and the local TV crew, forcing herself to keep her voice even so the tears wouldn't well up and spill over. "Dr. Abby Maitland has my profound thanks for making the birth process a wonderful, spiritual one. A new mother couldn't ask for anything more."

"What the devil is going on in here?" a male voice roared suddenly, drying her tears and stiffening her spine. The path of crew and reporters parted to reveal her long-lost husband.

Maddie faced Sam squarely, though the shock of seeing him again after all these months—and today of all days—made her knees slightly weak. "What's going on is a small media conference, Sam."

"Small?" He whirled to stare at the reporters, doctors and nurses clogging the room.

"Who's he?" an intrepid reporter called.

She stared at Sam's angry expression and cast subtlety to the wind. "The sperm donor," Maddie said brightly.

"The sper—" His furious eyes glared at her.

"Conference is over," Abby called, efficiently clearing the room, in command as always. "The parents need some time alone."

Maddie turned away. The last thing she needed was time alone with Sam. How could he have found out? She'd wanted to tell him in her own way, in her own time. When she'd known for certain everything would be all right with the babies.

The truth was that she'd procrastinated longer than she should have, not wanting to call the man who'd left her to admit she'd made a tiny withdrawal which had certainly paid astonishing dividends.

"How could you have kept this from me?" he demanded once the room emptied.

She put her hands on her hips. "How could I have told you?" Drawing herself up, she faked bravado to cover her racing heart. "You were in France. I was here in Texas. We haven't talked in nine months. There didn't seem to be a good time."

Maybe it was a lame excuse, but it was best to keep the past firmly between them. A barrier neither of them wanted to cross. The marriage was over, no emotions left to feel, no ties to bind—except these two babies.

"So they are mine?" He slung a curious, possibly frightened glance at the twin bassinets. "Your brother didn't make this up as a sick joke?"

Her stomach curled, tightening against the pain. "Are you saying Joey called you?"

"Yeah." A tic worked in his jaw. "Why were all these reporters and people in here? Was everybody supposed to know about this except me?"

"Sam, while I'm glad you're interested in the children—"

"Somehow you've made me a father. Didn't you think I'd be interested?"

Not in loving her, of course. In duty. "I prefer to think of your concern in this to be a minor one. We're separated. I won't be the first single mom in history."

"Just a mother with children she stole."

"I did not steal them!"

"I'm pretty sure I had some legal rights in this matter. You just can't take my...my—"

"Yes?" She raised her eyebrows, sensing his discomfort. "Sperm?"

"Stop saying that! It sounds so...clinical."

She went to the overnight bag she'd been repacking from her stay in the hospital. "It was a clinical procedure. I never thought of it as anything else." But she'd known he'd be unhappy, when he found out. Eventually, she would have told him.

When she'd found the right words.

"I can't move back from France right now. We're in the middle of a start-up project which has taken months to get into place."

"I don't remember asking you to return." She told herself it didn't hurt that he wasn't more amazed by the miracle which had happened. She didn't still love him. Would fight against loving him with everything in her broken heart. "Weekend visitation is all but impossible two continents apart. Don't worry. These are my children."

"And you expect me to walk out of their lives?"

A wheelchair was brought in. The nurse helped her into it. "Would you like to hold the babies, Ms. Brady? For the cameras?"

"Forget the cameras! This family is not going to be fodder for Ripley's Believe It Or Not, or Guinness Book, or whatever publicity stunt you're pulling. And the last name of those infants is Winston."

Maddie ignored the growl she remembered so well from the moment their marriage had begun to unravel. She was thirty-eight, and wanted children. He was forty-two, and hadn't felt the need the way she had. He was happy. She had not been. "Yes, please hand me the boys."

"Does using your maiden name not embarrass you? For them?" Glancing at the names on the ankle bands, he read, "Henry. Hayden." He grunted. "As much as I appreciate you at least naming these boys with our fathers' middle names, my name had better be on the birth certificates."

She smiled down into her babies' sleeping faces. "You're on there, Sam. If you'll excuse me, we need to return to filming."

"Filming? You're a movie star, now that you've robbed the bank?"

A stinging retort was on the tip of her tongue, but the nurse thrust the wheelchair handles into Sam's hands. "Mr. Winston, the reporters said that it would be a great touch if you pushed Ms. Brady out to the curb."

"Reporters be damned!"

"Interesting French you picked up while you were abroad," Maddie murmured.

"How do you expect me to feel?" he gritted out.

"Like a happy father?"

"I don't think so."

She could practically hear him grinding his teeth as he pushed her past a throng of people, clapping and waving at them as if they had done something special. Of course they had. This whole staff had invested their hopes and future medical hopes on her and her special babies.

"You only have to put up with us until you leave again," she said to him in a whisper, unable to hide a trace of bitterness.

"Did I say anything about leaving again?"

"I assume you will. Foreign investments and all that." She waved to a couple of nurses who had showed her how to bathe the tiny babies. And how to feed and care for them, one at a time and sometimes both at once.

"You'll need help. I don't see how I can go back for a while."

"Order your one-way ticket, Sam. Since your parents moved next door to me, I have all the help I need. Plus Joey's almost out of college for the summer, and is planning on helping in between football camps."

He stopped the chair at the curb, putting the brake on before stepping in front of it. "Did you say my parents moved in next to you?"

"Last month. Didn't they tell you?"

"Not exactly. They said they were moving to a

warmer climate, someplace where the winters weren't quite as cold. I thought that was a great idea. But I was thinking South Padre, not Austin.''

"Oh, well," she said brightly. "Austin is so much better than Amarillo, as far as they're concerned.''

"I guess so.''

She could tell he was very nonplussed by his parents' choice of residence. In a way she felt sorry for him. He *was* the last person on the planet who'd known about the babies. "My parents live on the other side, in the Reefer's old house," she said softly, as he helped her into the waiting limo the hospital had ordered. She had to speak softly because reporters were still running tape, the Maitlands were still smiling, blue carnations in green paper were pressed into her hand—and she so much wanted to appear like a normal family. No matter how much they weren't.

"Anything else you'd like to enlighten me on? Maybe just when you felt like I needed to know?''

She sensed his hurt and understood. "Would you like to ride with us?''

"I may as well," he muttered. "We're enough of a spectacle as it is.''

"I prefer to think of it as a circus. Active, bright, colorful, cheery. That's our family tree.''

"That's not how I'd describe a circus.''

She stared at the babies which were securely in car seats, one next to each parent. "Wave," she instructed. "With a big smile. Maitland Maternity has given us a future.''

She waved madly, smiling from the limo window as the car pulled away. Sam eschewed the all-is-right-with-the-world appearance. Absolutely nothing was right in his world.

He saw the delighted smile brightening his wife's pixie face, eyes glowing with happiness and pride as she called thanks to everyone on the hospital sidewalk waving goodbye to them—and knew nothing had been right since he'd left.

He missed the hell out of her. Unfortunately it didn't seem she felt the same way. She had everything she'd ever wanted now—and more.

"CAN YOU HEAR anything?" Sara Winston asked Franny Brady, who had her ear pressed to a glass held firmly against the closed bedroom door.

Tufts of Franny's iron-gray hair stood up a bit wildly as she leaned close to listen. "It's pretty quiet."

"Oh. That doesn't bode well." Sara pursed her lips. "Maybe Sam doesn't like the new decor. It's possible we went a teensy bit overboard with the Miami look."

Franny shook her head. "Maddie needed decorating with attitude. It lifted her spirits considerably."

"Has he gone into the bathroom yet?"

"I haven't heard any howls. Guaranteed if he didn't like the bedroom, he'll resist the oranges-and-bananas tropical wallpaper and—"

"Shh!" Sara didn't want to think about it. The pretty fountain they'd installed on the bathroom counter might not exactly be a hit. Of course, if they'd gotten the water to flow out of the statue's bowl instead of shooting from the woman's mouth, it wouldn't be so bad. "We may have some tweaking to do here and there. But all in all, I think we did a good job."

"Sure he'll be proud of how much we've tried to do in his absence." Franny pulled away from the door, and they went up the staircase to join the rest of the family. "Not that I mean to criticize your son, Sara. My daughter was just as much at fault."

Grandfathers Virgil Brady and Severn Winston rocked in matching white rockers.

"Where are the babies?" Franny demanded, seeing that the grandfathers weren't holding babies as they'd been when she'd left.

"Maddie came and got them for a bath," Virgil answered. "She said they needed a feeding and a nap. A second later, I heard the doorbell ring. Who was it?"

"Sam," Sara said grimly. "And he barely had a word to say to us! You'd think that boy could hug his mother after being gone so long. Not so much as the courtesy of a phone call to tell us he was coming back! But as soon as Franny told him Maddie was in their, uh, her bedroom, he headed in there so fast you would have thought bees were after him."

Maddie's nineteen-year-old college-linebacker brother, Joey, halted in the process of stacking diapers, putting away tiny infant clothes and carefully placing numerous baby gifts, which had been delivered to the hospital, on rectangular window seats around the nursery. "I called him," Joey confessed. "He knows what Maddie did."

"You called Sam in France?" Franny asked with a gasp. "When?"

"Yesterday. Someone had to tell him about the

babies.'' Joey's face was miserable. ''I don't think Maddie could. I think she had good intentions of telling him what she'd done, but as the months wore on, I think she got too scared.''

''We promised her,'' Sara said. ''Maddie's going to be angry. She wanted to tell him herself. She asked us just this once to let her handle her life. Oh, dear,'' she moaned. ''And yet I do believe you have a point, too, Joey. It did seem as if she never got around to making that call. I do believe in my heart that she was so distressed she simply froze.''

''Never mind that. There's a saying about playing the cards you're dealt. And Sam and Maddie have been dealt a pair of sweethearts.'' A pleased grin lit Franny's face. ''No wonder he was in such a hurry. I'd say that's a good sign.''

''Nothing to do but sit and wait for the explosion,'' Virgil said. ''Come here, woman.'' He gestured to his wife, and Franny went to sit on his lap.

Too refined to lap-sit, Sara took the window seat closest to Severn. They sat silently for a long moment, surveying the gentle decor and cheery blue and white train furnishings with pleasure. ''Now, this room we did right,'' Franny said.

''I agree.'' It was the room Sara had enjoyed redecorating the most.

''So, how are Sam and Maddie?'' Virgil wanted to know. ''Did you get to see them together before the boudoir door slammed shut? Did they rush into each other's arms?'' His sun-furrowed skin creased with hopeful expectation. Like his energetic wife, he wore faded, comfortable clothes much like he'd worn on the cotton farm they'd spent their long marriage working. Just as they'd worked the farm, Virgil and Franny were putting every ounce of their effort into seeing that these grandbabies had parents who lived under the same roof—even if they hadn't been under the same roof for nine months.

"I don't think that's exactly how it went," Franny said sadly.

"A bit of tweaking is all they need," Sara said. "I can tell our son still loves your daughter."

"Tweaking is good. Tweaking is important." Franny screwed up her face. "Maybe we should vacate to our houses so they can tweak."

Sara thought about that for a moment before shaking her head. "Let's just carry on as we planned. Sam left. Sam will have to adjust. If Maddie wants us to leave, that's different, but she might feel we've abandoned her in her hour of need."

"I hadn't thought of it that way!" Franny was aghast. "My daughter did feel deserted when Sam left the country. Although I'm sure he'd rather have stayed if they could have worked matters out. If he'd felt that she *wanted* him to stay."

"For the sake of these precious grandchildren, we must act as if nothing's changed. Even if everything has changed, from the decor to…well, you know."

The two women shared a conspiratorial glance. "Everything could change back," Franny said thoughtfully. "Maybe we haven't seen the last of the Brady-Winston miracles!"

"You said that right before you turned the fountain on," Sara reminded her. "We rigged that the wrong way."

"Well, the second time is supposed to be the

charm.'' Franny brightened considerably, jade-green eyes identical to her daughter's glowing with mischievous intent. ''This time, the plumbing is sure to work just fine!''

Chapter Two

"I feel like I've been hit by a two-by-four," Sam muttered as he stared at the two babies in matching bassinets in the bedroom he had once shared with his wife. "I'm a father!"

Maddie smiled as she stood beside him. "Aren't they beautiful?"

His almost-ex wife was beautiful. The tiny, writhing potato sacks with appendages he could only call astonishing. "I don't understand how you did this. How could you not have told me?"

He turned from the babies to the woman he'd been separated from for nine months. Was there a woman on the planet who could make him feel the emotions Maddie made him feel? Love, anger, desire, admiration—they all mixed together when he thought about her.

Unfortunately, right now anger was high on his emotional thermometer.

"Dr. Mitchell Maitland called one day to discuss a new, experimental procedure he thought might work well considering my age, and our history," Maddie told him.

Her cheeks pinkened a bit, but Sam told himself to ignore that particular trait he'd always found charming.

"I'm sure it's not too hard for you to understand that I leaped at the chance. And when I learned the procedure had been successful and that I was expecting, I didn't want you to come rushing back to America just because I was pregnant."

"Rushing back! We tried for five years to have children! Damn right I would have rushed back."

Maddie shook her head. "But what if it had just been another disappointment?" She lowered her gaze. "I couldn't tell you, Sam. I just couldn't."

He could feel his wife's pain. He'd felt it for months himself. The worst part was wanting a child—and wondering if he was the reason it wouldn't happen.

He reached to tip her chin up with a finger. "I would have wanted to be with you."

"I know. But anything could have happened, Sam, anything! And I…"

Her words drifted away, but her meaning did not. Sam took a deep breath. "I'm sorry, Maddie," he said. "I should have called you. Maybe I shouldn't have gone to France." He hesitated, knowing that wasn't even the beginning of what needed to be said. "We should never have separated. I think these babies are a sign we should have stayed together."

"I don't know," Maddie murmured. "I kind of think we needed some time apart."

Sam grunted, reaching into a bassinet. The baby boy looking out at him had his blue eyes but Maddie's hair color, the fiery hue of sunshine-dappled maple wood. When he touched the tiny fisted hand, the baby wrapped its fingers tightly around his, surprising him. A fierce protectiveness rushed into Sam's chest. "I'm not leaving you again."

"Sam." Maddie's tone forced him to look at her. "I don't know how to tell you this, but...I don't want to be the way we were."

He didn't like the sound of that at all. "Married?"

She nodded. "I mean, I know that technically we are, because we never actually filed with the court for divorce, but we did live apart for nine months. I feel like we aren't married anymore."

He held up a palm. "Don't say divorce to me right now."

"I'm not. But I don't want us to live together, either."

Shock filled him. "These are my children! You're my wife! Where else would I live?"

"I don't know." Her eyes filled with pain. "You're welcome to come by as often as you like, of course."

He stared at her, disbelieving. "When were you going to tell me about the babies, Maddie? If your brother hadn't called me, would I ever have known?"

"Yes!" Her face was stricken. "I would have told you. I meant to tell you."

"I should have been there. For you. For them." He glanced at the babies, their little heads poking out of matching blue T-shirts. "For all of us," he murmured.

They were chubby-cheeked infants, blissful in their innocence. One had gone to sleep quite contentedly. The other sleepily blinked his eyes at his new world, which wasn't quite in focus.

Surprise, surprise.

And now Sam and Maddie had what they'd always wanted. Actually, had what they'd wanted times two.

But she didn't want *him*. Or their marriage.

Okay. Three was a crowd, but four made a family.

He was going to romance her socks off until she clearly saw that Mommy needed Daddy, babies needed Daddy—and a wife needed her husband by her side.

To love, honor and cherish, for better, for worse.

"MARTIN, LISTEN." Sam rolled his eyes as he stared at the ceiling. Talking to his lawyer required having a better handle on the chaos that had become his life; his grip had slipped disastrously. "I know you didn't know I was planning on having children. The point is, I have them, and I need you to draw up a will that includes them."

"I heard you, Sam. And as your lawyer, I have to advise that you have appropriate tests run before you assume Maddie is correct about your paternity," Martin insisted. "Don't get your butt in a sling just because you've let the guilt squeeze be applied to your heart. Think with your wallet."

"My wallet pays your salary," Sam reminded him.

"And I earn my salary by protecting your interests," Martin retorted. "I'll do anything you instruct me to do, Sam. And you know how much I like Maddie. It damn near killed me to have to think about drawing up divorce papers. You know that! She's like everybody's kid sister.''

"Not mine."

"Okay, half the male population sees her in a kid-sister light. The other half would kill for just five minutes to kiss the lace of her underwear.''

"I will assume you are in the first category, unless you want your head removed from your shoulders,'' Sam said dryly.

"Definitely, buddy,'' Martin answered hastily. "But that's what I mean. I hated to see you lose her, especially when I know there are multitudes of clowns just waiting for a babe like her. But now I'm telling you to cover your bases. Not that Maddie's lying. What if the test tubes got scrambled in the lab or something?''

"What are you saying? That my kids could have problems and I shouldn't provide for them?''

"I'm saying don't you want to know for certain that this Maitland clinic got your genes mixed with Maddie's before you take the serious step of changing your will?''

Sam digested that for a moment. "No."

"Why not?"

"It wouldn't really matter to me, Martin. Maddie and I talked about adopting kids at one point, anyway. The process was long and arduous, and we didn't make it through many of the steps before…'' Before he'd snapped under the pressure of not being able to give his wife what she wanted. *And now she's done it, without me. She's the only woman I've ever loved. What difference would adopted children or my test-tube results make? She loves them. And so will*

I. "Why should I have tests to establish paternity? Just to find out those aren't my babies? Call me a dreamer, Martin. I don't want to find out they're not mine. I'd rather assume I'm just chock-full of egg-seeking, healthy, tough, indestructible sperm. Do you mind?"

Martin sighed. "You know, your ego is skewed. Most men would need to know that their money wasn't being used to take care of another man's progeny. You? You just want to get Maddie back."

"I want to believe I can have progeny," Sam growled. "Ego cost me my wife. Smart men learn from their mistakes."

"I know," said Martin. "That's why I keep you on as a client, even though you don't listen to a word I say. You're a good man, and a lawyer ought to have one good client who isn't looking for a loophole."

Sam frowned. "Speaking of loopholes…"

"Oh, boy," Martin said. "Don't make me cry, Sam."

"I may not be the hero you think I am. Get out the tissues. I haven't been feeling very heroic lately." Mainly, he felt like he'd let his sons down by not being present at their birth. *I shouldn't have left Maddie to her own devices. I let my pride overrule my heart.*

"I've known you since high school. It's tough to suffer any illusions about a guy who used a jock strap as a slingshot in the locker to defend me from the A-string army. I became a lawyer to protect you from any and all litigation your bad humor got you into from that day forward."

"It was only a few overdeveloped knot-heads who needed to be taken down a peg. You could have used your own jock strap if it had been bigger."

"Great. Always the personal jibes about the short, skinny guy," Martin complained.

"But you don't owe me your life from that day forward," Sam told him gently. "I merely want one simple thing."

"Name it," Martin said, as always.

"I want to find out how I keep Maddie from dipping into my sperm savings in the future. I have rights in this matter, and I want them exercised. I know she wants more children. Four was always her dream number. I just don't want my name in the father slot on her future lab experiments."

Martin coughed, and it sounded like whatever he was drinking spewed everywhere. "You really are giving up the hero role, aren't you, buddy?"

"Yeah. I still want it friendly and easy, the way you managed to work out the specifics of our separation."

"Kid-glove detail."

"Exactly."

"Why do I have a bad feeling Maddie isn't going to want to be my stand-in little sister after this?"

"Maddie believes I only want to be here for the sake of the children. She's never going to be convinced that I want her for her, and that I honestly believe we belong together. Any future children are going to have to come from our physical—"

"I think I get your drift," Martin interrupted. "I'll get right on it."

MADDIE STARED AT her mother and Sara, who'd come in to help her with diaper time. Then she burst into tears.

"What's wrong, honey?" Franny demanded.

"I don't know. I'm weepy for some reason." Maddie touched the toes of her babies lovingly, each touch a miraculous sensation she cherished. "I think seeing Sam again has me off balance. This should be a happy day, and yet he's angry with me. I expected him to be upset, but I didn't realize how strained we would feel." It had been so much better when she and Sam had enjoyed a happy marriage. To see him again after nine months had been a shock to her system. His anger had been heartbreaking.

Each grandmother took a child in her arms. Franny shooed Maddie toward the bathroom. "Take a shower. You'll feel so much better if you do. A good warm shower will wash all those worries away."

"All right." Maddie sighed and went to get some fresh clothes. She was in between sizes. Her pregnancy clothes were too big now, and her regular clothes didn't fit. She pulled out another pair of elastic shorts and a sleeveless top that would cover a nursing bra. "At least this gives me the illusion of working toward my normal body size."

Franny eyed her over the sleeping baby in her arms. "Don't rush yourself. I know you're feeling tense with Sam right now, but I'm sure he finds you attractive just the way you are."

"Men always think of your body the way it was before the baby," Sara assured her. "At least Severn always says he still sees me as the girl he fell in love with."

"Maybe that's the trouble. Sam's not in love with me. He'd live with me again, to give the children a proper family. But any deep feelings we had went out the window during our marriage." Even though this had been a fact for a long time, Maddie still found it wrenching.

"He didn't seem angry to me awhile ago," Franny said. "Although I did hear him raise his voice a bit when he was on the phone."

"Must have been about the wine company merger," Sara guessed.

"I think he was talking to Martin," Franny said with a frown.

"Oh, well. That explains it. He always yells at Martin." Sara shook her head as she finished diapering a baby. "It's not a normal legal relationship those two have, that's for sure. I don't yell at my lawyer. He's too…uninvolved for me to yell at. I say what I want, and he does it."

"Well, Sam never did what anyone wanted him to," Franny asserted. "And Martin merely does his best to advise Sam, who is usually intractable, and I mean no insult to you and Severn. Sam is Sam and I'm sure he had Martin's head in a vise for good reason. Now, dear, I'm positive Sam is simply trying to come up to speed on the fact that he's a father, and he's not angry with anyone."

Maddie wanted to believe Franny's words, yet was painfully aware of the wounds their marriage had suffered. "Mother, haven't you ever heard the old saying there's no going back?"

"Nope. Haven't heard that one. I have heard that the second time's the charm," Franny said brightly.

"I don't know. Something's not right," Maddie murmured. "We're not on the same track anymore. Sam and I used to be compatible. We were very comfortable with each other. We're just awkward now." She glanced up at Sara and Franny. "Out of whack."

"Out of whack?" Sara repeated.

"Not on the same wavelength," Maddie clarified. "I have a funny feeling Sam called Martin about the babies."

"Maybe he wanted to brag," Sara suggested.

"Not if he was yelling. And that's what makes me nervous. Sam never yelled before. He's a very civilized person."

"Well, Martin could drive a body to yell," Franny pointed out.

"Custody agreements can't be instated at this point, can they? Since the babies came after our separation?"

"Oh, Sam wouldn't want to take the children away from you," Sara said. "He wouldn't think it was right for a mother and her children to be separated."

"Well, they're not just her children," Franny said slowly. "As much as she thinks she did it on her own, she did require help. And that help was Sam's doing. Reckon he has some rights where the boys are concerned. Maybe he just wants to know for sure, and that's why he called Martin."

"Oh, dear," Maddie said. "I wouldn't want my babies going to France for their visitations."

"I'm sure Sam would let you come along," Sara exclaimed. "Wouldn't that be fun? The two of you and the children in such a romantic place?"

"You're not helping," Maddie said gently. "Sam and I do not want to take trips together."

"Sam and I don't want to do what?" Sam asked as he entered the room after briefly knocking.

"Don't want to go to France together," Maddie explained.

"No. We wouldn't want to do that," he concurred. "I just told Martin to rescind the offer to Jardin Wineries. I need to be here with the boys." He looked fondly into the baby blanket Sara held and spoke soft gibberish to his son.

Sara and Franny both sent triumphant smiles at Maddie, before quietly exiting the room.

"Glad we got that all straightened out," Maddie grumbled, not glad at all for some reason. In fact, now she felt grouchier than ever. Sam being around all the time meant he'd be underfoot all the time. She'd expected him to pop in and then pop out of her life.

It appeared he planned on staying. Her heart rate elevated, the blood singing through her body in giddy anticipation.

"And I also instructed Martin to draw up a will that includes my children. I want to make certain they're taken care of should anything ever happen to me."

Maddie's blood stopped cold. Here she'd been thinking about Sam trying to obtain custodial rights, and he'd been thinking of the children's well-being. "Oh, Sam," she said. "You are a good man."

"Not really." His expression was a trifle sheepish. "I was just explaining to Martin the difference between a louse and a hero."

"You're not a louse."

"Sometimes I am. You're just seeing everything in a rosy light because you've just been through the miraculous process of birth. Amazing that little fellows like these can grow from…" He shook his head in silent, awed admiration as he stared over at his sons.

"I think I'm the louse," Maddie said sadly. "I was thinking all kinds of bad thoughts about you when they told me you'd been on the phone yelling at Martin."

"I yell at Martin when he aggravates the hell out of me, which he does frequently. He wants me to have the babies' DNA matched to mine, in case there was a screwup in the Maitland blender."

"Oh." Maddie's brows rose. "I would be very surprised if Maitland made a mistake such as that."

"I told him it wouldn't matter to me, anyway. You had those children, and you love them. They have my name on the birth certificate. If they're not born from my cells, then it's no different than if we'd adopted. Martin understands this now."

"Oh, Sam." Her eyes sparkled at him. "You have no louse potential at all."

"I do," he assured her. "I also told him I didn't want any more withdrawals made from my account."

Maddie lowered her head after staring into Sam's eyes for a moment.

"Well, I wish you felt differently, of course. But I certainly understand."

"You do?"

"Yes." She nodded. "And when I'm ready to have more children, I'll have Dr. Abby help me select another appropriate donor. Of course, I doubt there's a man alive who could give me better children than you, but I certainly—''

"Maddie!" he bellowed. "You are not running a stud farm around here!"

"Sam—"

"This entire discussion infuriates me!" He glared at her. "Pardon me for having an adverse reaction to the idea of you blithely shopping for sperm!" He took a deep breath and glared at her again.

"Well, I'm not planning to try to become pregnant for quite a while, anyway. So there's no need to be upset."

"Until you leave one afternoon to go shopping. I won't be thinking Neiman Marcus, I'm sure," he grumbled.

She put a hand on his arm, and instinctively he reached to take that hand in his. When she realized he'd done it out of habit, reacting comfortably as he had hundreds of times before, she stiffened, then relaxed. It felt right to let Sam hold her hand. Their marriage had been close and loving. He was a good man, even if he had a slick lawyer. "I'm going to take a shower. Our mothers say I need to relax."

"You definitely need to slow down. You keep me turning in circles."

"I don't mean to."

"Don't you?" He eyed her carefully. "Somehow I thought you were enjoying torturing me."

"No." She shook her head. "Not torturing. Although the occasional good-humored teasing does bring to your eyes a fire I remember well."

He sank onto the bed, his shoulders slumped.

"Just don't let me find any lists lying around for a while, unless they're for the grocery. Okay? And even then I'll be doing the shopping for quite some time."

"Safer that way?" she asked with a smile.

"I was thinking of your recovery, but yes, possibly it is safer if I know you're tucked at home recuperating."

He was still holding her hand in his, and warmth spread through Maddie. But she wanted to make certain he understood the whole situation. "Sam, you know I want more children, don't you? I mean, if heaven smiles on me with more babies, I would consider it a dream come true."

He looked up at her suddenly, his eyes full of the fire she loved. "Fine. Have four. Have ten. But just let me take a crack at getting you pregnant the old-fashioned way."

Chapter Three

Sam had no idea why he offered. What was he saying? That he accepted that Maddie wouldn't be his true wife, but a sexual relationship designed to create more children was fine with him? "I mean, if we were to have a real marriage, of course. I would be very vigilant with practicing."

She tipped her head to look up at him. "Practicing?"

"Well, I couldn't shoot out any arrows that hit the bull's-eye before. Maybe I just needed more practice."

"One thing I can never say about you, Sam, is that you were unskilled and out of practice."

"I may be, after nine months."

She smiled hesitantly, her face taking on a glow that spoke of happiness. "That almost sounds like a confession."

"A confession of what?" He stared at her, confused. "Oh…you're asking if I've been *totally* out of practice since our separation?"

She turned away. "It's really none of my business. I read more into your remark than I should have."

Yeah, but it had made her glow, and he liked that. Gently, he turned her to face him. "Yes, Maddie, it was a confession, even if I didn't realize I was making one. There has been no other woman since you."

She stared into his eyes, searching. Maybe she was trying to see his feelings. Surely she didn't have to look so hard. He leaned forward to drop a soft kiss against her forehead.

"It shouldn't make me so happy," she said, her voice trembling as she leaned against his chest, her forehead resting at his throat. "It does, though. And that makes me so angry!"

"Why?" He held her away from him a little so he could see her face.

"I don't want to love you anymore," she said, sniffling. "I don't want to sound mean, but it took my heart a long time to heal, Sam. Actually, it never has. It's kind of hanging in my chest, a big, gaping wound that I don't think will ever stop leaking sadness over our breakup. I just can't go back there."

"Back where?"

"To the hopes and dreams," she said softly. "It was too hard when we couldn't work things out. I learned the true meaning of heartbreak when I couldn't give you children."

"But I—"

"I know you didn't want them as badly as I did. But substitute the baby issue for a different issue, Sam, and maybe I'll let you down again. I don't have any confidence in myself as a wife."

"I was happy."

"But that was the only real big issue our marriage

was even tested with. What if something bigger came along?''

He wasn't sure there was anything more momentous than not being able to get his wife pregnant when she wanted to be. ''I think I see what you're getting at. I felt the same way about not being able to give you something you desperately wanted. But just for the record, I didn't have any complaints.''

''No, you didn't. It was all my fault. I was the one who wanted children, and that destroyed our marriage.'' She sighed and pulled slowly from his arms. ''I caused us pain.''

''I have to shoulder my share of responsibility, Maddie. I shouldn't have told you to choose between our marriage or the continual merry-go-round of fertility heartache. Those are words I can't unsay, no matter how much I wish I could. Of course, I was expecting you to pick me.''

Maddie shook her head. ''If I'd been any other woman, I would have. That's the whole problem. I'm selfish.''

''You're sweet, too. A man's got to take the bitter with the sweet. Vinegar and sugar is probably a good recipe for something, isn't it?''

''Salad dressing.'' She crossed her arms thoughtfully, before meeting his gaze. ''Not much nutrition in that.''

She was talking about nurturing their marriage. Sam nodded. ''Guess nothing in life is perfect, Maddie. I like you just the way you are.''

''Yes, but you're a better person than me, Sam, really. You want to have a marriage again. You'd want to try to make a baby with me. All this because

I didn't tell you I was trying to conceive without you here. It isn't right if you're the one who always does the compromising.''

"I'm just thinking what's best. We've got two little babies to consider, and I want us to give them a good family. Two happy parents.''

"You've given up France, and your wine company,'' she pointed out. "You'd looked for the right deal for a long time.''

"I think my life will be better in the long run if we merged Sam with Maddie in Texas. All I can think about right now is babies who need their father as well as their mother.''

"It's so uneven,'' she murmured. "Like the new shutters on the house. They're lopsided, Sam, but only because Mom and Dad didn't agree on what was even. She'd say up a little, he'd say no, they should be down a little, and the house ended up a little off balance.'' She gave him a pain-filled glance, her delicate brows drawn together. "A little here, a little there all adds up. Somehow I think we'd end right back at square one.''

"You need some time to yourself,'' Sam said softly, "and I think you said a shower might be relaxing. So I'm going out to visit with the extended family. Try to get some rest.''

She nodded slightly, her lower lip quivering, her eyes big and haunted as she watched him close the door behind him.

Outside, he hesitated, thinking about what they were doing. About what they weren't doing.

She had never planned on him returning for good.

He wished that didn't bother him as much as it did.

"IT'S NOT THAT WE DON'T want you here, Sam," Sara Winston told her son as she walked him over to see her rented house. "We just aren't set up for company. We've been spending all our time helping Maddie with her house. And in the final months of the pregnancy, she didn't feel so well. In fact, she was housebound. Severn and I thought you'd want us here in Austin to help in any way we could."

"I'm hardly company."

She glanced away for an instant. "You know what I mean, surely. The only bed in this house is ours."

Hard to argue with that. He was their only child, so it wasn't like they'd ever plan for extended visits from farflung children. Except him, and clearly they had neither planned for nor expected his return. That didn't make him feel one bit better. "You could have mentioned that your new address was next door to my ex-wife. I thought you were retiring to the coast."

His mother adjusted her pearls. "Maddie told us this house had come up for rent, and Severn suggested we take a short lease to see how we liked the area. We weren't certain, you know, if Maddie would get tired of having us around. To tell you the truth, Sam, it's so much nicer being close to her. Otherwise we would be spending our time in hotels or hauling up and down the highway to visit. This way we avoid a great many sleepless nights and purposeless worrying from not knowing what was happening here. And we've had the time of our lives getting to know

Maddie and the Bradys better. In fact, your father is seriously considering purchasing the house for our permanent retirement residence.''

"That doesn't explain why you didn't tell me.''

"Maddie didn't want us to, and we agreed, Sam. You can be angry if you like, but we did what we thought was best for you and Maddie.''

"Unfortunately, there is no Maddie and me.''

"Certainly there is. They're named Henry and Hayden, and that's all your father and I care about. We didn't choose sides. We chose to live near our grandchildren and their mother.''

He kissed his mother on the cheek. "Thanks for looking after Maddie.''

"You should be next door with the children, anyway. Not over here with us.''

That wasn't the way Maddie wanted it, and he'd decided to do things her way—for now. "It's all going to work out, Mom. I'll see you later.''

He left the house, intending to go back to Maddie's.

"Sam!''

He straightened at the carrying sound of Franny Brady's voice. "Yes, Franny?''

She gestured from the porch of what had last been the Reefers' house. "Let me hug your neck, Sam. You haven't given me a proper greeting.''

"Let me make up for that at once.'' He sprang up onto the porch and gave her a sound, grateful hug.

"Now, you bad boy. You come inside and tell your old mother-in-law what was so pressing in France that you had to run off and leave us all in the lurch.'' She went inside the comfortable one-story dwelling, leaving him to follow.

''Maddie and I agreed to separate,'' he began in self-defense as she pointed him to a chair in her mahogany-paneled kitchen. ''She wanted it just as much as I did.''

Franny put a paper plate on the table in front of him, loading it up with brownies and butterscotch cookies, then thumped down a glass of tea beside his plate. She stared at him from under iron-gray curls tumbling over her broad, lined forehead. Franny was from sturdy farm stock and didn't tolerate guff in anyone. Her daughter had inherited a great deal of her head-on attitude. ''You knew when you married my daughter that she wasn't like any other woman. You always said that. Said she was original. That you wouldn't find another like her if you hunted the world over. So, how's the hunting?''

''I haven't been hunting. Maddie is Maddie. One of a kind. But Franny, I couldn't give her what she wanted, and it was difficult.''

Franny's face softened. ''I understand how hard that must be for you, Sam. But I think you jumped the gun. And damn it, I hate to lose the only man I'm positive I could stand for a son-in-law. Truly.''

That touched him. He'd gotten along very well with Franny and Virgil—once they'd accepted him. They hadn't thought he'd be happy with their daughter, suggesting that perhaps his family was too embedded in the Silk-Stocking Row for him to know a thing of quality when he saw it. He'd known it, however. Maddie would sparkle no matter where she was, and growing up on a hundred-acre cotton farm hadn't affected her brilliance. "I can't change the fact that we separated. Can't turn back the clock."

"No. But it would be best for everyone if you cease this disastrous living arrangement here and now. The two of you belong together. And I hope you'll remember my advice and not get all hotheaded when you discover Maddie decided to return to using her maiden name." Franny shook her head. "I sure wish you the best of luck, Sam, but quite frankly, I fear you stayed away too long."

MADDIE NEARLY HAD heart failure when the door to her bedroom was flung open. She instinctively tightened her hold on the baby she was nursing. "Did it ever occur to you to knock?"

"I just had a conversation with your mother."

She frowned at her tall, way too handsome ex. "I'm trying to relax so I can breast-feed. I can't deal with family angst right now."

He sat on the edge of the bed, his gaze suddenly fixated on the contented newborn at her breast. Plainly uncomfortable, he diverted his gaze, fastening it to the lamb-and-lion picture on the opposite wall. "I beg your pardon."

"Not necessary. Just please don't barge in. This is the only place in the house I can be alone. I'm having trouble letting down."

"Relaxing?"

"Letting down milk."

"Oh." He moved his gaze to a large potted palm in the corner.

She closed her eyes, enjoying the feel of the warm,

sleepy baby in her arms. "Are you bothered by the breast-feeding?"

"I'm not sure what I am. Trying to give you some privacy, I think." He stared down at his hands. "I'd like to help, though."

"What do you want to do?"

He shrugged big shoulders, the white polo shirt he wore flexing over a broad back. "Help somehow. Hold the baby. Do something. To be honest, I'm having trouble letting down myself."

They weren't talking about milk now. "In what way?"

"I guess even though those are my children, I don't feel bonded to them in any way. Connected."

She could see the frown of concentration even with his face in profile. "You weren't here, so you didn't see me pregnant. And you haven't really held them. Go ahead, Sam. Pick Henry up."

"Where is he?" He looked around, finally spying the baby between two king-size pillows on a towel on the lace-covered bed.

The small baby lay on his stomach, sucking his fist gently, eyes blinking. "I don't think I should pick him up. I might hurt him."

"You won't." Maddie smiled. "It's the only way to bond. You have to touch them, hold them, smell them. Change diapers."

She stood, handing Hayden to Sam before he realized what she was doing. He was too busy trying to figure out how to settle the tiny baby in his arms to sneak a look at her breasts, and Maddie thought it an excellent sign that he was concentrating. Silently, she picked up Henry and settled him to feed.

Apparently Sam developed the knack of holding a baby with lightning speed because his gaze immediately focused on the infant latching on to her nipple. Rats. Now *she* was uncomfortable.

"Your breasts are so swollen. Do they hurt?"

"A little," she admitted. "Though I think I won't be in as much pain if you look away."

He did, but she could see his eyes were still wide with amazement. The tingling between her legs warned her that she was still very aware of Sam as a man, not as her ex. She insisted to herself the physical sensation was only her body reacting to the baby suckling her nipple. *Abby told me that breast-feeding would cause my uterus to contract. That's all it is.*

"I like holding him," Sam said, his voice rich with pleasure.

Unexpected tears popped into Maddie's eyes. Would miracles never cease?

"You're kind of…sweet," he murmured. "I mean, I think you need a diaper change, little fella, 'cause I'm pretty sure that's not baby powder I smell, but hey, a guy's gotta do what a guy's gotta do, right?"

He held the baby to his chest, gazing down into the small, open eyes. "I think someone should clean your bottom, which is going to be a little cruel since you've had your nice warm mother comforting you with those big breasts, treatment to put any right-thinking male into a seriously relaxed trance. A wipe down to the backside won't be near as nice, but then you can get right back inside your cozy little blanket. Quite the life of luxury, eh, little man?"

Maddie's lips parted as Sam oh-so-carefully laid the baby on the bed.

"How do I do this?"

Her eyes widened. "Can you?" She'd expected him to hand the baby to her.

"Is there a huge difference for babies?" Sam asked. "Except less space to cover?"

"I guess not. The washcloths are stacked on the bathroom counter. Go in there and warm one up, and grab a diaper, too."

"Okay." He went into the master bath. "Whoa! Who installed the ugly woman spitting water? That's frightening!"

Maddie grinned. "Our mothers."

"Ugh!"

"It's supposed to be soothing. They put it in there to give me an illusion of tranquility. Your mom read that the sound of water bubbling or gurgling was supposed to be calming, so my mom bought the fountain, and together they worked on it."

"I'm sure they had the best of intentions." He brought the warmed cloth out, and carefully peeled off the tiny diaper. "I didn't hear any bubbling or gurgling. Just spitting. And I've got to tell you, that's not a remarkably serene sound effect."

Maddie couldn't help laughing. At that moment, her milk let down. "Oh, my gosh!"

"What is it?" He stared at her, pausing in his diapering.

"I let down! I let down! It really works!" Grateful delight ran all through her. "I was so afraid I wouldn't be able to breast-feed!"

"Why wouldn't you? You've got more-than-satisfactory equipment."

She let that go in her joy. "I don't know. I just was afraid I couldn't." Staring at the baby suckling earnestly now that he was being rewarded for his trouble, Maddie smiled in dizzy relief. "I got nervous when I couldn't let down. And there are all these people in the house, which I love, but it's…"

"Hard to relax."

"Yes! And then there's the formula cans."

Sam finished diapering the baby and cradled him to his chest as he sat on the edge of the bed. "Formula cans?"

"Well, there's so much pressure, Sam! I know this will sound neurotic, but it says right on the can that 'breast milk is best. But if you choose not to feed your baby breast milk,' etc. etc. I mean, how is that supposed to make a woman feel?"

"Pressured?"

"Exactly! I couldn't get pregnant the normal way. What if my other equipment failed me?"

"I don't think that's possible."

She missed him staring at her breast, which was free of the towel she'd draped over her shoulder. "It all just made me tense, I guess. I'm so happy I can breast-feed my babies!"

He shook his head. "I think you should kick everyone out of the house, except me. This is time you should spend relaxing."

"I have privacy in my room, and our moms have decorated it beautifully. I'm supposed to feel like I'm in a jungle, far away from everything, among the natural elements of life."

"It's certainly got that primitive feel."

She shook her head at him. "I must have relaxed when you made me laugh, enough to let down."

"Glad I'm good for something."

"Precisely. Because if anyone had told me you'd be the instrument of my relaxation, I would have been very concerned."

"Stranger things have happened, I guess. Why don't I diaper that greedy little guy if he's through, and you three can take a nap?"

She narrowed her eyes at him. "Why are you being so caring?"

"I was always caring, Maddie. I simply want us to go back to what we had before." He helped her up and toward the bed, taking the baby from her. "You know, *our* natural element."

Tucking Henry next to her body, she said, "Our primitive instincts."

"Well, yeah. I mean, we'd gotten so calendar-happy. It's tough to get passionate when you feel like you're playing beat-the-clock. Not that I'm complaining about having sex. Just the performance thing started to weigh on me." He glanced at her. "I knew I was letting you down. And when the doctor mentioned my potency, I knew I was holding you back from what you wanted most. That's not what marriage should be."

"Oh, Sam." She stared up at him, feeling regret for everything. "I am sorry about all that."

"Well." He finished wiping and diapering Hayden and tucked the infant next to his mother. "Good to see that I wrung out some powerful babies, after all."

"You did." A slight smile curved her lips. "Dr.

Maitland told me there was a major explosion in the old petri dish.''

Sam nodded at her, not believing a word but enjoying having his vanity soothed. ''You know, this is the first time I think I've related to you how insecure I'd been.''

''Oh, Sam, I never thought you were the problem. I thought it was me! It's terrible not to be able to give your husband a child.''

He rubbed the back of his neck. ''You with your breast milk hang-up and me with performance anxiety. We should do something about our neuroses.''

''We did. It's called separation.'' She closed her eyes sleepily, lulled by Sam's deep, comforting voice.

Sam looked at his wife and the two content infants hogging the king-size bed, a threesome he wasn't invited to join. He sighed and went to sit on one of the striped chairs. ''So, Sam,'' he thought to himself. ''Everything's in good working order now. What next? What's the opposite of neurotics who separate?'' He laid his head back against the chair back, pondering the ceiling. ''Secure people who stayed married to each other.''

Maybe. Trouble was, Maddie had already given him a definite no to that suggestion. She was probably right. She was happy now, as she'd said, and more than anything he wanted her to be happy. ''Hey, Jane,'' he murmured softly, ''any room in your jungle for this Tarzan?''

The phone rang, startling him into an upright position. He snatched the china floral phone, answering it so Maddie wouldn't waken. ''Hello?''

"This is Dr. Abby Maitland. May I speak to Maddie Brady, please?"

He resisted the urge to growl Maddie *Winston.* "She's asleep."

"Is this Sam?"

Well, at least Dr. Abby knew the origin of the sperm. "Yes, it is."

"How's my patient?"

"Doing fine."

"How are you doing?"

He frowned at the physician's interest. "I didn't just give birth, so I'm not the one you should be concerned about. Maddie is. So if there's anything you can tell me about how to make this easier on her, that would be appreciated. Any special dos or don'ts?"

"She needs lots of rest and TLC," Abby said. "A healthy diet, lots of fluids. No lifting except for the babies, of course, and no sexual intercourse for six weeks."

"Ah." Six weeks! "I'm so happy I asked."

"I'll just bet you are." Abby laughed. "Don't hesitate to call me if you have any other questions. Please mention to Maddie when she wakes up that I'd like to speak with her."

"I'll do that. Thanks."

"You're welcome."

He heard the laughter not concealed by her professional tone, and hung up the phone, highly disgruntled. Maddie turned over on the bed, her legs smooth and gleaming in the afternoon sunshine lighting the room. He bit his lips and drummed on the sides of the chair.

Six weeks! Thank goodness he'd already warned himself that until he and Maddie worked things out, she was hands-off to him. But oh boy. There was no question he was still desperately attracted to her.

Sam was an old-fashioned guy. If any more of his children were destined to be born, they weren't going to be stirred in a petri dish or shaken in a tube!

The only way future babies were going to be whipped up would be by him and Maddie finally getting together—naked, skin-to-skin and primally synchronized.

Made the old-fashioned way.

Hide in your jungle, Jane, because Tarzan has no intention of being left out again!

Chapter Four

"You're taking care of yourself, Maddie?" Abby asked.

Sam had given Maddie a message to call her doctor after she'd awakened from her nap. He'd been pretty careful not to so much as touch Maddie's fingers when he handed her the portable phone. She sighed, remembering days when Sam had never avoided her. "Even if I weren't, there's an army here to make certain I take care of myself."

"How is Sam coping?"

"Sam is Sam," Maddie said, her voice even. "Always the gentleman."

"Hmm. Annoying, is it?"

Maddie laughed. "Maybe a little. Him being a gentleman makes me feel like a witch. I've brought all of this turmoil on myself and him, too, but he's so nice about it that I've got guilt growing like a weed."

"As your doctor, I must advise you to stop thinking like that, Maddie. It's not healthy. You can't relax if you're letting yourself have it all the time. Sam is trying to help."

"I know. But I can't help thinking that if he were just a bit less of a prince, I wouldn't feel quite so witchy."

"It's not normal," Abby said with a sigh, "for a man to be so much more prince than frog, is it?"

"No! It's not!" Maddie laughed, thankful for Abby's insight. "And I don't like feeling as if I'm the frog in the story. But that's it. I'm an overweight, warty frog."

"I suspect that's very contrary to Sam's way of thinking. If a man gives a woman all the love and kindness and consideration he can, shouldn't she be happy? Shouldn't she feel like a princess?" Laughter colored Abby's tone. "Mix that with after-pregnancy hormones, and you've got a real emotional cocktail for Sam."

Maddie smiled. "Do you know any man who offers to change diapers? Go grocery shopping?"

"Not many. But maybe—maybe, Maddie—you deserve this handsome prince."

"We weren't happy before."

"Then don't think about getting back together just yet. Play it by ear. You'll have no expectations to meet. Goodbye, guilt. *Pfft!* Just like that."

"That won't make Sam happy. He wants a traditional family. And he doesn't want me hitting the test tubes again," Maddie said slowly. "He wants to try to have children the, um, coital way."

"Sometimes the floodgates open after a pregnancy, Maddie."

Her heart lifted at that piece of good news. "Do they really?"

"Oddly enough, yes. In fact, many women get

pregnant after giving birth much more quickly than they would like.''

''Oh, my.'' Maddie's heart started pounding at the thought of her big, handsome husband inside her again. Lovemaking with Sam was wonderfully addicting. Pleasurable memories gave her skin goose pimples. ''Sam has princely tendencies in that area, too,'' she said, her tone wistful.

''Doesn't feel so bad when you think about those good old days, does it?'' Abby asked with a laugh. ''Six weeks, please. And I'll need to see you in two.''

''But what if it doesn't take?'' Maddie asked. ''What if my floodgates don't open?''

''I can't assure you that they will,'' Abby said, ''but two babies are enough if it means you and Sam are happy together. Everybody's got to compromise a little. I'll see you in two weeks, and in the meantime, let that gorgeous husband of yours pamper you. The nurses here have talked about nothing else since they laid eyes on him the day the twins were born. Just like that Mason Blackstone. My goodness, he's certainly turned the place upside down. I believe he could get raffled off among the nurses.''

''Those twins are fine, then?''

''Yes, thriving, I'm happy to say. Mason's a lot like Sam, just as devoted. There're a lot of disappointed ladies around here. Too bad Sam only had eyes for his wife,'' she said. ''We should all be so plagued. Ta-ta, dear.''

The line went dead as Abby's cheery voice faded. ''Goodbye,'' Maddie said slowly, turning off the portable phone. Maybe Abby was right. ''Maybe I'm really not a frog,'' she murmured. Perhaps just overly cautious. Neither she nor Sam had been happy at the end. But her soul had twisted when Sam said he'd expected her to choose him.

She hadn't expected him to actually walk out of their marriage. And then leave the country.

For nine months.

It had hurt so much. He didn't have to go so far away. She had thought their marriage was finished. And now he wanted to walk back into her life. She understood he was motivated by the babies, but it hit an off note in her heart that he'd had no intention of coming back for *her*.

She thought about Mason Blackstone, and his vigilant care of the twins he'd found himself unexpectedly fathering. They'd been born a scant two hours after Maddie's, so she'd followed their progress with interest. Mason had been with those babies every second upon discovering he was their sole guardian. Sam was reacting the same way Mason Blackstone had upon finding himself in a paternal role. He was being protective. Caring. Sheltering.

It was an instinct she appreciated but selfishly, she wanted more. She wanted Sam to have returned to her without knowing about the children. She wanted Sam to have never walked out that door. She wanted him to have stayed in America.

She wanted all the doubt to go away. She wanted forgiveness to rush into her soul, instead of guilt.

No matter how hard she tried to keep him at arm's length, he was determined to sneak back into her heart. Yet the equation was lopsided.

Secretly, she was hurt that he'd talked to Martin

about keeping her from using his DNA. She wouldn't have hit the sperm bank again without discussing it with Sam, and she felt he should have known that. Or talked to her about it. They were running on different tracks, or maybe she expected his trust when she didn't deserve it.

But a real fear underlay the hurt she was hiding behind. Walking into the bathroom, she stared at the water fountain their mothers had tried so hard to build. Despite their best intentions, it hadn't quite worked out right.

"Okay," she said to the curvaceous metal woman that adorned the fountain. "Say that Sam and I put the past behind us. But then we can't get pregnant again. I don't think that would be good for Sam's ego, especially since I've conceived without him."

She dabbled her finger in the water that pooled at the bottom of the statue's skirt. "I could compromise. I could say that two babies are all I want, although Sam probably wouldn't believe me at this point. And he's already ruled out any further lab experiments, as he puts it." She sighed, wondering if she could trim the picture of the large family she'd always dreamed of down to two. "Maybe my skin *is* green and warty," she said to the spitting woman.

The water *fitz-fitzed* unabated.

"Suck it up, sister," Maddie told her. "You're not exactly perfect yourself."

THE PHONE RANG as Maddie stepped from the shower. She picked up the portable she'd left on the bathroom counter. "Hello?"

"May I speak to Mrs. Sam Winston, please?"

Puzzled, Maddie frowned at the foreign accent. "This is Maddie Winston."

"Maddie, my name is Vivi Jardin. I hope you will not mind my phone call."

Her stomach dropped; her heart began an uncomfortable pounding in her throat. "I hope I don't, either."

"I would not have called, except you are the only person who can possibly help me with my problem," Vivi said.

Maddie pulled her towel more closely to her. "What problem would that be?"

"I do not know if you are aware of this, but your husband has canceled his plan to buy our company, Jardin Wineries. Did he mention that to you?"

"Briefly." Maddie wasn't going to discuss Sam's business dealings—but she wasn't going to correct Vivi's use of the term "husband," either.

"It puts my brother, Jean-Luc, and me in a terrible position, to be honest. We can't find another buyer on such short notice, and as much as I hate to say this, we find ourselves financially embarrassed. We were counting on Sam to buy our company so we could pay off creditors, you see."

"I think you should speak to Sam about this."

"Well, that's the problem. According to his lawyer, Sam wants to concentrate on matters at home, specifically his two children." Vivi's voice lowered silkily. "We understand that. We wonder if perhaps we could lure you into having a honeymoon vacation in our country, where you could see our wonderful vineyards, and perhaps get an idea of everything Sam is giving up?"

Maddie stiffened. *Giving up.* During their separation, Sam had told his parents this winery was the chance of a lifetime. Now he'd given up his dream, when she had selfishly coerced him into hers. She hadn't meant for that to happen.

If Joey had waited one more day to call, Sam would have what he'd worked so hard for. His dream.

No, that was all wrong, too. Sam had the right to know about his children.

"It is not uncommon for companies to woo the family of the prospective buyer," Vivi continued. "We are aware that Sam has a family with needs that must be considered, and we are prepared to work with you, if there is any chance at all you believe Sam might still be interested in purchasing us."

Oh, there was no question he'd be interested. Sara had said that Sam was like a kid in a candy store over the possibility.

"This deal is important to us because Sam is an interested foreign buyer, you see. And he has the financial resources, as well as an international reputation for his business acumen and knowledge of the industry. Jean-Luc and I were only too happy to have an American buyer who would help us with our cash flow problem, and yet allow us to maintain our name and company position."

"I see," Maddie said slowly.

"Is this something you might consider? We would be more than happy to arrange a vacation here in lovely France for you and Sam, and a tour of our vineyards."

"I could mention your idea to Sam," she said reluctantly. ''I don't know that I have any sway with him.''

''Thank you,'' Vivi said. ''You would like France.''

''Oh, I couldn't come, though I appreciate the invitation,'' Maddie replied, distracted. Her nipples started to tingle and burn, surprising her. She was letting down on her own! It was time to nurse her babies. ''I'm afraid that's too far for me to travel right now.''

''What a shame,'' Vivi said softly. ''France is such a wonderful country. So romantic.''

''Yes, I've heard. Goodbye.'' She switched off the phone and hurried to the audio baby monitor, which she snapped on. The sound of crying reached her ears. ''Mom?''

''No, it's Sam. Are you all right?''

''I'm fine, but I think the babies need to…need me.''

''I think you're right. I'll bring in the troops.''

By the time Sam entered with two wailing babies, Maddie was seated in a striped chair. She took one from Sam, cooing to it as she put it to her breast. The baby latched on with no problem, sucking hungrily. Maddie beamed with joy. ''Did you see that?''

''Uh, yes I did.'' Sam shifted, keeping his finger tucked into Hayden's mouth so the baby would be pacified long enough for his brother to feed. ''Pretty amazing.''

''Yes, it is.'' Maddie felt like she sparkled all over with pride. ''What good boys they are!''

''Their mom's pretty amazing herself.''

Amazing? Not really, when she had so many

doubts about almost everything these days! But she could push herself, for Sam's sake. "I just received a very surprising phone call."

"Oh?" He looked at her, and Maddie thought he was so handsome. The truth was, she wanted him all to herself, but that wasn't right.

"Vivi Jardin called."

"Vivi!"

He didn't look pleased. Maddie pushed away the jealousy and reminded herself to be amazing. "She is upset that you rescinded your offer."

"Then she needs to discuss it with me."

"I told her that." She swallowed, brushing her baby's cheek with a light finger. "She said that she and her brother wanted to bring me over there to see the vineyards. Apparently, the Jardins are in some financial difficulty, and want to hang on to you as a buyer. She made no bones about wanting to romance me as part of the package."

"If I want you romanced, I'll take you to France myself." His frown deepened.

"I don't want to poke my nose into your business, Sam. But wasn't this something you wanted?"

"Past tense."

"The only reason you changed your mind was the babies, right?"

"Not exactly."

His eyes shifted, and she knew he wasn't telling the truth. Her heart felt as if it were turning inside out. "I'd like to see you achieve something you want," she said softly. "I know how much it means to finally have what I always hoped for." She stared down at the pretty baby, her soft, plump dream come true. "I'd like that for you, too."

"Maddie, I'm focusing on you and the children right now. Everything else is peripheral."

I cost him that. Selfishly. He'd had no choice in fatherhood. "Sam, it's too uneven."

"I'm happy, Maddie." He stared at her. "I don't know what else to tell you."

She closed her eyes. *Sure you are. You're just thrilled that I stole your dream.*

Chapter Five

"I'd just like to know what Maddie's supposed to do with all this wine," Franny complained to Sara. She stood with her hands on her hips, surveying the growing collection of French wine bottles. Severn and Virgil each held a bottle, examining them with longing. Joey sat at the kitchen table drinking beer and playing solitaire.

"Boo-jo-lay," Virgil read. "Sure is a pretty bottle. Don't believe I've ever had any Boo-jo-lay."

Sara shook her head. "Now is not the time to start. Maddie said we couldn't open the wine because she feels funny about accepting gifts that are designed to get her to try to change Sam's mind. We need to respect her feelings."

"That was when it was only one bottle," Severn pointed out. "Now there's two weeks' worth. I say it's a shameful waste of good grapes to let them sit. Why don't we open a bottle, just to let it breathe? Maybe Maddie would be tempted then."

"Maddie's nursing," Franny said. "I don't think all this romancing from Jardin is going to do any good, since Maddie can't drink this much wine. But don't try to excuse yourself by saying the wine shouldn't stay in the bottle, because everyone knows wine gets better with age."

"Yeah, but not me. I'm feeling puckish." Virgil set the bottle down, sighing. "We'd better get started building a wine rack," he said to Severn. "Fourteen bottles of wine, delivered at the rate of one a day…how big do you consider the rack ought to be? We could end up with enough to have a block party if that Jardin woman keeps trying to convince Maddie to help her out with Sam."

Severn squinted at the ceiling. "Let's go with a floor-to-ceiling job, about four slots wide. If that doesn't cover it, we'll plead with Maddie to let us drink the overflow."

Franny sighed. "I don't think it will do any good. She's determined to stay out of Sam's business. Matters have been very strained since that Frenchwoman called."

"Nah. Matters got strained when Sam started sleeping on the couch in the nursery," Severn said.

"It was hard to tell my own son he couldn't stay with us," Sara said, her voice trembling. "Are you sure we're going about this the right way, Franny? I know the plan was to try to squeeze them together, but it seems that Sam and Maddie are further apart than when he was in France."

Franny plunked down on a stool. "They were together at her two-week checkup, weren't they? I thought it was a good sign she allowed him to take her."

"Only because he said he'd ride on the back of the car if she let Joey drive her to her appointment!"

Franny looked at her friend. "She doesn't want to be beholden to Sam, but that *was* carrying it a bit too far. I don't know why my daughter's got herself in knots over that wine company. If Sam wanted it, he'd buy it. Wouldn't he?"

"Well, yes, but he wanted it before he found out that Maddie needed him. Of course, she doesn't think she needs him, and that's the problem. Or maybe she doesn't want to need him, so he'll go back to France. Actually, I don't think I understand Maddie at all. And I wish she would have left the babies with us. That's what we're here for. To help her. And so is Sam. But she hardly lets anyone do anything for her, and I think it's very unappreciative of her!"

Franny thought Sara might be about to cry. "It does seem that the situation is a bit out of kilter."

"I'm sorry to say this, Franny, but I think Sam's jumped through plenty of hoops to please Maddie. Now, you know I love her as if she were my very own daughter, but I think she needs a good talking to!"

"You offering?" Franny asked. "I hope you are."

"You're her mother!"

"That doesn't mean I've ever been able to make her see sense once she had her mind made up. Maddie's always had to learn from her mistakes."

"I think she's making a big mistake now."

"Can't make a gal do something just because he wants her to. It's never worked that way with love before, Sara." Franny tried to be reasonable, but her lid was starting to jump from the steam building up inside her head. "Just because he wants it don't mean she's gotta do it."

"It's just so hard to see him so unhappy!" Sara wailed. "Shut out from his own family!"

"Let's focus on how we can bring them together, not get upset about them avoiding their marriage. After all, no one knows what goes on behind closed doors."

"Very little in this case," Sara said sadly. She shredded a paper towel with agitated fingers. "Franny, my heart is breaking! I know he's a grown man, but he's still my son, and I hate to see him in pain! It makes me hurt all over just to think about it."

"Well, here. Wine's medicinal, isn't it, Joey?" Virgil reached for the bottle of Beaujolais. "As Maddie's father, I say it's time we do some taste-testing. I'm sure Maddie wouldn't want you suffering unduly, Sara, not when the cure is just waiting to have its cork popped."

"Now, Virgil—" Franny began.

"That's an excellent idea, Virgil," Severn said, joyfully picking up a chardonnay with a lovely label decorated with fruits and scrollwork. "I wasn't in the mood to build a wine rack, anyway."

"I'll do bar duty," Joey offered, "since I'm experienced in bar tending at college."

"Since when? You're on an athletic scholarship." Virgil eyed him distrustfully.

"Football players get to eat pretty well, and the guys like a firm burgundy with their steak," Joey stated.

"Oh, dear," Franny said, the last of the extended family to acquiesce. "I mean, don't you think, er, that is…" She glanced around the granite island counter in the kitchen, where people and wine bottles were now grouped. "Maddie said—"

"Maddie's not here. After her check-up she's going to show off her babies to the hospital staff, and fit in a fast look-see with the pediatrician. We've got a couple hours before she comes home, not that she'll allow us to help her much then, either," Sara said grumpily. "I wouldn't complain if she stays gone with Sam all day."

"Now there's something to think about," Franny said thoughtfully. "Maybe they just need a date. A dinner date!" She clapped her hands. "Sara, you're brilliant!"

"I'm afraid to ask what you're thinking."

Franny ignored Sara's comment. "Let's set up a table just for the two of them, with the crystal candlesticks and a tablecloth. We'll put a bottle of red wine on the table. Then we can steal over to my house with the babies, and they can enjoy an evening alone!"

"That will work until the babies need to be fed," Sara said.

"Oh, pooh. I forgot about that." Franny frowned for an instant. "Well, no plan is foolproof. We'll just have to go with it."

"I'm all for it," Severn said. "But what about us? Do we all vote to pop some corks or not?"

Everyone looked hopefully at Franny. "Um…" She hesitated. The faces grew glum. Briefly, she closed her eyes, before opening them wide with innocence. "My nerves *are* a trifle stressed from all this planning. How about we head out to the patio and have a steadier or two?"

Instantly, everyone grabbed a bottle and hurried out to the patio. Corks popped, wine breathed and glasses clinked. They each fell into a chair or onto a chaise lounge.

"Now this is the life," Severn said happily. "French wine, on a sunny May day. Mmmm-mmm! It doesn't get any better than this!"

"TRY TO DO BETTER than that!" Maddie told Sam with irritation. "It doesn't cost so much to call France. You used to do it all the time. You call Vivi Jardin and tell her we're shipping back every single bottle of that wine." Maddie hurried from the doctor's office, the good news about her weight and general health spurring her into a long-overdue discussion with Sam. "You've made your feelings plain about staying in Austin, and that's fine. I don't want any more wine sent here to change your mind, though. Tell her your answer is still definitely no, and that I don't drink, so all the effort is wasted." Actually, Maddie loved a glass of good wine, but this wine was exported from France with intent.

"I'm not calling Vivi. Martin can do all the phoning."

"Maybe there's some other reason why you don't want to simply call and tell her that if we receive any more wine we're going to float away."

"No. I would think two weeks of samples is probably enough. I'm sure you've seen the last of it."

"She'll call me again. You know she will. All these wine bottles mean she's got her fingers crossed that I'm working on you. And then what do I say?"

"Now is not the time for me to acquire a company." Sam held a baby carrier over one arm as he followed her down the hall. "These babies need me. Most importantly, you need me, whether you want to face that or not."

The ride home was fairly silent, except for an occasional squeak from a baby in the back seat. Maddie felt very skittish about all the wine arriving daily from France. The negotiated business deal was important to Jardin, but also to Sam, although he didn't want to talk about it much.

"Home sweet home," he said, pulling into the driveway.

It wasn't really. Having Sam around had made the last two weeks the longest of her life. She alternated between wanting to kiss him and wanting to scream at him. Abby told her it was the hormones, but Maddie was pretty certain it was chemistry other than that. Unresolved tension.

She pulled out Henry's carrier, and Sam took Hayden's. Together they walked inside, marveling at the quiet coolness. "Isn't it amazing how the house settles down when the babies aren't in it?" she asked. "It's so peaceful."

Sam walked into the kitchen. "Uh-oh. Be careful with your adjective."

"What does that mean?" She followed him into the kitchen, her jaw dropping. Fourteen wine bottles sat on the center counter, ten open. "Oh, for goodness sakes!"

"Guess I can't return these to Vivi now."

She set the baby carrier down and crossed to the sliding door, which led to the patio. "Look at them out there! Sleeping like babies!"

Sam came to stand behind her. "Ah, the models of responsibility."

Her mother lay on a lounge, her head lolling back against the headrest, her mouth open toward the sky. Her father was draped next to her, his head on her chest in a familiar fashion they would normally never have displayed in public.

"It looks like the god of wine crash-landed in our backyard," Maddie whispered. "We were only gone three hours, too. You think they could have stayed out of mischief!"

"Look at my parents," Sam said in disgust. "My dad's got his hand up my mother's skirt."

Maddie gasped. "No, he doesn't! At least not the way you make it sound. For heaven's sake, Sam, it's a tea-length dress! His hand can only be on her…her knee."

Perhaps it was his mother's thigh, but Maddie wasn't going to upset Sam further. She was humiliated enough by Joey. He'd loosened the top snap on his jeans, maybe to better improve the circulation of wine through his blood. He looked like an underwear model who made a career out of eating. "I'm going to have words with my brother! Look at him! Do you think that patio table was built to hold two hundred-and-fifty pounds?"

"It was designed to hold plastic plates and light drinks with toothpick umbrellas floating in them. But doesn't he look happy, all sprawled out there, shaded from the sun."

"He looks drunk!" Maddie snapped. "I should have known that Vivi would peddle the most potent wine in the world."

"Yes, but what a nice dinner we're apparently having, Maddie. Look at this romantic table setting. A rose, good china and the sterling."

She stood beside him, and Sam felt regret wash over him for the days when they'd taken a romantic evening for granted. "I think they're trying to do something nice for us."

"They're trying to do something all right."

Her voice was stern, but Sam knew she remembered the better days of their marriage, too. "Seems a shame to waste all their effort," he murmured, gently taking her in his arms. They hesitated, unfamiliar with the feel of each other at first before their lips fused, then touched again, molding to each other in a good old-fashioned kiss even the French would appreciate, Maddie thought wildly.

She stayed still in Sam's arms, wishing he wouldn't stop kissing her. She had missed him so badly! Why, why was he the only man she could be attracted to?

Relaxing against him as he kissed her cheek, along her neck, to the hollow of her throat, Maddie moaned.

He stroked down her arm to take her hand in his, laying it against his chest. "I missed you."

"I was thinking the same thing."

"You won't hate me in the morning then?"

She laughed. "I don't think so. I couldn't regret a kiss like that."

He nuzzled her ear, biting lightly at the lobe. "I feel like I've got a buzz myself."

"Now you know why your dad's got his hand up

your mom's skirt, and it isn't solely because of the wine.''

"Don't talk to me about it." He ran his hands up Maddie's back, tracing her bra strap. "How is this all supposed to come out?"

"What?"

"You. Me. The babies. This."

She closed her eyes again, seeking relief from his gaze. "I don't know. I'm scared."

"Funny, I feel the same way."

"You do?" She gazed up at him. "Scared of what?"

"Oh, little babies who cry and I don't know why." Moving the hand he held to his lips, he kissed each finger. "My wife terrifies me, because she changed everything while I was gone, and I do mean everything, from furnishings to the number of bodies in the house. She's got no place in her life for me. And I think I should apologize for a lot of things, but I'm scared I won't say it right, and even if I could, all the I'm sorry's I could say would fill the ocean between here and France and maybe still not be enough.''

"Oh, Sam." Trapped by everything she was feeling, she stared into his eyes, her heart tapping against her throat. "Let's not be sorry anymore. Let's just be a family."

"Like that?" He jerked his head toward their reclining relatives.

"Yes. Just like that. Wouldn't it be nice to be so comfortable with each other we could simply relax like them?"

He looked down at her. "Are you saying you're not relaxed with me?"

"You make me very nervous. How can I be kissed like that and not be?"

"Five years of marriage, Maddie. We know everything about each other, or we should."

She frowned. "Maybe we shouldn't."

"Are you keeping secrets?"

"No." Moving away slightly, she said, "Not anymore. But I did. And I'd do it all over again, the same way. I'm sure you wish I wouldn't say that, but it's true."

"I wouldn't." He tugged her back into his arms. "I'd install a tracking device on you."

"What?" She couldn't help smiling at his teasing tone.

"Well, now I realize I should have been keeping up with your every move while I was gone. When Joey called me, I was shocked."

"I still haven't had my chat with Joey about that. Where were you when he called you with the big news?"

"In a restaurant."

"Mmm. In France. That sounds romantic."

"It wasn't. It was business."

She glanced up at him as he held her in his arms. "With Vivi?"

"Yes, with Vivi. We were trying to finalize the deal."

"Ah, so close. No wonder she's upset." Maddie leaned her head against Sam's chest, smelling the familiar scent of him she'd always found so sexy. And sometimes so secure. "Maybe I should have installed a tracking device on you, if I'd known you'd be squiring beautiful women to romantic dinners."

"I would not consider Vivi a beautiful woman."

She lifted her head. "I saw pictures of her and her brother in *Wine* magazine. She's stunning."

"Not to me. You're confusing outer beauty with inner beauty. Vivi can be a shark, I'm pretty sure."

"Oh, I don't like sharks. They bite." She snuggled back against his chest, relaxing. A delicious languor was stealing over her, and she didn't want the mood to go away.

"Yes, they do. As I told Vivi, I never mix business and pleasure." He ran a swift hand under Maddie's skirt, giving her bottom a lingering massage.

She jumped, moving swiftly away. "I'm taking the babies upstairs."

"That's not an invitation, is it?"

"No." She laughed. "It's avoiding temptation."

"Where's Vivi's wine when I need it?"

"It wouldn't help you," she said. "I'm unavailable for another four weeks, and even if I weren't, I wouldn't."

He followed after her with the baby carrier she'd left behind. "Four weeks is a long time. You might change your mind."

"Nine months was a long time. We'd made up our minds, though. Without the babies, we wouldn't be having this conversation right now."

Setting down the carrier in the nursery, he glanced around the room, assessing it. "It looks different without all the family cluttering it up like the Waltons."

"We are certainly not the Waltons!" But she laughed, just the same. "You aren't John Boy by any stretch." *Way too sexy for that.*

"I doubt Ma and Pa Walton ever tied one on, either. Somehow I think it should be us on the patio, forgetting our cares."

Maddie sat in a rocker, and Sam took the one next to hers. The babies slept on, undisturbed by the emotions their parents were feeling. "We must have hurt each other a lot, to have drawn up those separation papers," she said softly. "I don't ever want to go through that again."

"I don't, either."

"But we did the right thing, Sam. You know we did." She rolled her head to look at him. "I could kiss you all night and it would be wonderful, but in the morning, I'd still be glad we're separated."

"Not me. I'd be going for seconds. And thirds."

She smiled. "You obviously haven't spent a night up with the babies if you think you'd actually want sex. Would you like to do an all-nighter?"

"Not the kind you're apparently suggesting, but will you get some rest if I do?"

"I'm ready to give the boys up for a night. I could chill some breast milk for you."

He leaned close, taking her hand in his as he stared into her eyes. "I'll make you a deal. You send all of our relatives off to their various dwellings, and I'll be Dad on duty. Empty out this place so it's just you and me, and I'll be more than happy to watch late night talk TV. And reruns of *Twilight Zone*. With the babies."

"You think you can?"

"I'm more than up to the challenge." He pounded his chest, Tarzanlike. "And if I do it without any assistance at all from anyone, I get my reward in the morning."

"Hey! I don't get a reward for doing it!" she said, jumping because his hand was sneaking up her skirt again. "All you're going to want is a nap after that."

He leaned close to whisper in her ear so their sons wouldn't hear. "I want to kiss your ankles," he murmured.

Every tiny hair along her arms became electrified. "Is…that so?" she asked carefully.

"And your calves."

"That would be a great place to stop."

"Not until I get to your thighs," he said silkily, taunting her ear lightly with his tongue.

"And then you'll stop? It really is the place to stop," she told him. "You noticed your father respected the Mason-Dixon line."

"Yes, but I'm an international traveler. And I'm used to different time zones, so I know I can stay up all night, and then kiss you all over in the morning."

She gasped, her heart pounding, her nipples tight as rosebuds. "Sam—"

"I think our parents have the right idea. A romantic evening with great steak and fabulous wine, just the four of us, two who are little enough for an early bedtime. Don't you find that tempting?"

It was difficult not to agree with him when her blood was singing to the tune he was playing. Common sense told her it was a bad idea—her nearly ex-husband and seduction were a *terrible* combination—but having her ankles kissed was so enticing…. "It sounds anything but relaxing," she said, making her voice as stern as possible. "I thought you said I needed to relax."

"You'll feel like melted butter before the sun hits the noon high, I promise."

"Maddie!"

Franny's voice suddenly shattered the mood. Maddie jerked away from Sam, pulling her hand from his grasp.

"Yes?"

"Oh, my goodness!" Franny rushed into the room, panicked until she saw the babies were asleep. "We noticed your car was back," she whispered urgently. "We…we must have dozed off."

"We noticed."

The rest of their family filed upstairs behind her, and suddenly the large nursery seemed very small. Their faces were pink from the sun, and perhaps from embarrassment. They were slightly sweaty. Joey had buttoned his jeans and stood shaking his head like a sleepy bear trying to clear away buzzing bees.

Sam squeezed her hand. Maddie bit her lip, trying to decide.

He ran one finger casually along her ankle as he leaned over to surreptitiously adjust a baby blanket.

"Listen, everyone," Maddie said in a rush, "we're giving you the night off. Sam wants to try staying up with his sons so everyone can rest."

Sara clasped her hands together. "Oh, Sammy, I'm so proud of you."

"That's my boy. Responsible," Severn said.

"You'll grill the steaks and sit at the table we set for you?" Franny pleaded. "We were trying to do something nice. We didn't mean to fall asleep on the job.''

"It's okay," Sam told her. "You all deserve a break. And Maddie's in very capable hands. Trust me.''

Chapter Six

"Wimp!" Joey observed, staring down at his zonked brother-in-law. An unmerciful glee lit his eyes. "Guess staying up all night with two tiny babies was more than old Sam could handle."

"Take it easy on him." Maddie thought even an exhausted Sam was handsome. Dark brown hair lay rumpled on his head. A dark shadow stubbled his jawline and lower cheeks. His chest was bare, and she tried not to think about how fit he was. But a lean washboard stomach and nicely developed chest was enough to make any woman look twice, and she wasn't just any woman. She was still his wife, technically—looking was okay, right? She gave herself permission to look again—and caught Sam staring at her.

"Good morning," he said.

"Good morning." She refused to let the rush of admiration panic her into acting less than cool. He'd nearly talked her into letting down her guard last night. She'd nearly surrendered to Sam's seduction.

Thank heavens the babies wore him out!

"Guess I missed the fun. Sorry about that."

She shook her head. "Don't be." She picked up an infant, refusing to be lured by Sam again. "I haven't slept that well in months."

"Glad to hear it."

"So am I," Joey interjected. "Maddie didn't sleep well from about the middle of her pregnancy on. And in the beginning of her pregnancy, she hurl—"

"That's not necessary, Joey," Maddie interrupted. "Sam doesn't want to hear all the gory details."

He raised an eyebrow as he lounged on the sofa. "Maybe I should."

"It's not that interesting."

"I think I might find it more interesting than you give me credit for."

She wasn't going to allow the intimacy to build between them again. Last night had proved to her that Sam's power of persuasion was still very strong. "I'm going downstairs to breast-feed Hayden," she said, picking up the baby.

"I'll bring Henry in a few minutes," Joey told her. Since Henry was still sleeping, and Hayden was ready for a meal, Maddie left without glancing back at Sam.

"So. You were going to fill me in on some details Maddie feels I don't need to know?" Sam raised an eyebrow at the man who outweighed him by at least a hundred pounds, but who was gentle as a kitten except for his love of body-bruising sports.

"I guess not. I've already betrayed my sister more than I should have." Joey sank onto the sofa next to Sam, picking up the TV remote to flip through channels.

"I'm glad you called me, Joey. I'm not sure Maddie intended to anytime soon."

"Yeah, well. We all worked on her about it. But she swore our folks and yours to absolute secrecy. And we could see she was totally tortured with panic that she might not be able to carry to term." He shrugged massive shoulders. "Right or wrong, we decided to let Maddie call the shots in her life, not that we've ever been much for minding our own business before." Joey rolled his head on the sofa to give Sam a piercing look. "In case you wondered, we didn't take sides when you two split up. We kept thinking Maddie would break down and call you herself. But," he said with a sigh, "she was paralyzed, and I suppose I can understand."

"So why'd you finally break down and tell me the good news?"

"Because Maddie was so sad. She was afraid to call you. Afraid you'd be angry, and afraid you wouldn't want to come back." Joey stared at him, his big eyes honest. "You'd been gone an awful long time. She'd accepted that it was over. But in her heart, I think she wanted you to come back on your own. It would have broken her heart if you weren't happy about the children."

"I'm happy," Sam growled. "I'm so happy that I'm trying to talk her into having a real marriage again."

Joey nodded. "Well, Maddie's a tough case, no question. I think she's pretty determined to not need you anymore."

"I see."

Getting to his feet, Joey laid down the remote. "Guess I'll shove off. There's nothing on the tube."

"Did you come by just to gawk at my stupor from being up with the twins?" Sam stared at his brother-in-law narrowly.

"Yeah. I needed a good laugh today."

"Thanks." Sam grimaced.

"Aw, don't feel sorry for yourself. I know you deserved it, 'cause Maddie told me you saw me stretched out on the patio table yesterday. And laughed because I'm such a lightweight drinker."

"It's the only thing you're a lightweight at," Sam grumbled.

Joey rolled up a burping towel and tossed it at him like a football. "I'll let you get back to sleep. See ya. Come on, Henry. Time for din-din."

He scooped the infant carefully in his huge hands, much like he would a football he was recovering, and went downstairs, thundering on the steps though they were carpeted. Sam stared at the blank TV, thinking about everything Joey had told him about Maddie.

They'd been happy together. What more did two people need other than love and respect?

He'd let his ego get in the way, and that was all there was to it. And Maddie was determined not to get hurt again. He could understand that. There was plenty of time to devote to winning her back.

No time like the present. He hopped up, pulled on a shirt, ran a hand through his hair and went downstairs to find her.

She was in the kitchen, hanging up the phone as he entered. She smiled as he picked Hayden up from a nearby blanket. "Are those sons of yours starting to wrap you around their little fingers?"

"They are awfully cute, I have to admit." He sighed, his chest expanding in a manner Maddie found very appealing. "When they're not crying. That's a bit rough."

Her eyes widened. "Did they cry? I didn't hear a thing."

Sam shifted, sending a glance at her out of the corner of his eyes. "You may not want to hear this, but they only woke up once. After they drank up their bottles like greedy pigs, and a speedy diaper dance, they went down like stones."

She put her hands on her hips. "You get night duty from now on. They've never slept through the night for any of us."

She could tell he liked that by the grin he wore.

"It's because I'm their father. They sense security nearby."

"Oh, I see. Good. I like sleeping at night."

Sam's forehead wrinkled. "Henry doesn't quite eat with the enthusiasm that Hayden does, though."

She'd noticed the same thing. "I try not to let it worry me. He was last to be delivered, and they had a little tougher time with him, so maybe his appetite isn't quite as developed." She was rationalizing, she knew, but Henry's appetite did worry her.

"So, about the morning's activities you escaped before I had a chance to make good on my promise—"

Maddie held up a hand. "Not to hurt your feelings or anything, but with the dawn came rational thought.

I realized just how bad of an idea it would be to succumb to your offer.''

He raised a brow. ''Oh?''

''I need to be thinking clearly,'' she said primly. ''About our family, about us. I can't be involved in a pseudoromance with you.''

''Pseudoromance?''

''We're not on, but we're not off,'' she pointed out. ''That is, if I let you, um, romance me. I want to stay off. It's better for me that way.''

''Not for me.''

Maddie stared at him, unwilling to say another word. He was handsome as the devil, he could say all the right words, but she had suffered too much up to, through and during their separation to allow herself to forget all the pain. Maybe it wasn't right not to be able to move on, but their marriage breaking down had hurt too much. ''I'm sorry, Sam. I think I'm handling all I can right now.''

''I'd like to be there for you. I'd like to be an emotional support.''

She shook her head. ''I have to do this for myself.''

''Why? Why won't you let us do this together?''

''Because the first thing you did when you got back in town was tell Martin to file papers to ensure I stayed away from what you consider yours,'' she said. ''As simply as if it were only wine bottles. First, you called Martin to rescind your offer. 'Draw up the papers, Martin, and tell Jardin the deal is off.' Then you called Martin to keep me out of the sperm bank. 'Draw up the papers, Martin, and tell Maddie the deal is off.''' She snapped her fingers. ''Everything is business to you, Sam. When you want something done, you bring in your heavy. Martin.'' Opening her purse, she withdrew some papers and slapped them against his chest, so he instinctively reached up to grab them. ''These were delivered to me this morning. Pardon me if I don't wait around to see what papers you're going to have me served with next.''

She hurried away, tears blurring her eyes.

''Maddie! Hang on a sec!''

Sam grabbed her arm, slowing her down before turning her to face him. ''Hey,'' he said, wiping the tears away gently from under her eyes. ''Believe it or not, I've already had an epiphany this morning about how I've been handling the situation.''

''What kind of epiphany?'' she asked, trying to hold back a sniffle and not succeeding.

He shook his head as his fingers continued to stroke along her cheek. ''A Joey epiphany.''

''Oh.'' She snatched a tissue from a box and scrubbed at her nose. ''About what?''

''Not fitting into the picture. When I received the startling news in France, I guess I came home with certain ideas of how I thought I should handle the matter. Though I was thrilled to be a father, I knew you well enough to know you'd be back at the lab conceiving—without me.'' He paused, his eyes searching hers. ''I want you to need me, Maddie. I don't think you'll try to fit me completely into your life if you have someplace else to go for what you want more than anything.''

''Joey needs to mind his own business. I don't want you having any epiphanies,'' Maddie replied, her voice crisp. ''I may be too reliant on Maitland, but you're definitely too reliant upon Martin.'' She stared at Sam, her eyes flaming with anger.

"I'll admit it was the wrong thing to do. I do feel sort of misplaced, or not needed, in a crazy way I can't understand. I'm sorry. I'm trying to fit us together, Maddie. Don't you want that, too?"

She hesitated for a moment, staring up at him. The blood rushed through her body, pumping hard through her heart, making her feel nervous. "It's not you. It's me." She took a deep breath. "I've invited Vivi to visit, Sam. I called her this morning, and with the time difference, she was able to get a flight for today. She'll be here around seven. I've called Martin and invited him to dinner, so you'll have your legal beagle on hand for the paperwork. I want you to buy her company, and then I want you to go back to your home in France.''

Chapter Seven

"What?" He pulled Maddie to sit on the kitchen table bench. "You're serious about all this, aren't you?"

"Yes, I am. It's no good, Sam." She looked at him sadly. "We are what we are."

"It was good enough before."

"No, it wasn't. You know that. You're trying to act like the past never happened. It did, though."

"I don't care about the past, Maddie. I care about us. I'm not going back to France."

"You'll make me very unhappy if you stay. You're trying too hard, and I'm uncomfortable with trying to force our marriage back together."

He sighed. "You're right. I have been moving quickly. I guess I wanted to fit us together for the sake of Henry and Hayden, and to do that, I felt like I needed to make up for lost time."

Her eyes crinkled at the edges wistfully as she looked at him. "I still love you," she said softly. "I always will. But we hit that fork in the road, and we chose different paths. I want you to go back to

France and stay on the path you were walking before Joey called you.''

"Well, I really can't. There's a giant tree down, blocking my path. So now I'm walking across the tree trunk, balancing carefully, to get over to your path, which is clear.'' He walked along her arm with his fingers, until he reached her shoulder. "Good thing I'm possessed with natural athletic ability and flexibility, because my destination is here.'' And he lightly tapped her heart. "This is home.''

She didn't want to smile. It wouldn't be good to encourage her husband's teasing. "Joey's been certain he was right about everything since the day he was born. If you keep listening to him, he'll convince you to follow his pigheaded example.''

"No way.'' Sam tugged her to her feet. "You'll never catch me flat on my back on a table under the patio umbrella. Let's steal Joey's motorcycle and take a ride. The folks won't mind watching the babies. Who knows? I may even decide to buy myself a Harley. For that matter, if you get the hang of it, I'll buy you one. A matched set. We could put a baby carrier on each one, and motor the babies to the beach occasionally.''

She stared at him, her eyes huge.

"Oh, you *like* that idea.'' He reached out to stroke her cheek.

"No, I don't! It would be reckless and immature!''

"Hmm. Right now, yes. But later on when they're old enough to wear helmets…come on,'' he said softly. "Who better to find yourself with than your husband?''

"There's something very wrong with the noun in that sentence."

He took her hand, and this time she let him. "Nah. 'Finding yourself' and 'husband' both refer to healthy life phases and happy memories from the past. That's a good thing. We can learn from our mistakes. Kids like Joey don't know everything." While Maddie glanced away, Sam stuffed the papers from Martin into a kitchen cabinet. "Let me call the folks over."

Ten minutes later, Sam helped Maddie onto the motorcycle. Then he assisted her with the helmet. "Now, you're going to have to put your hands around my waist, and avoid all cracks about how that's in the past, too."

"The thirty-two inch waistline, you mean?" He was as fit as ever, but Maddie sensed he was attempting to put her at ease.

"Exactly."

"My old waistline is pretty much history, too," she sighed. "The twins pulled me every which way."

"Now that's a true regret I have." He put on his own helmet, staring at her as he did. "I wish I'd seen you pregnant."

"It wasn't a pretty sight. While the experience was like one of the wonders of the world, I'm afraid I wasn't very attractive."

"I doubt that." He got on the bike and reached behind him for her hands. "I hear they call these love handles," he said, placing her palms on his waist. "So love me, baby."

She rolled her eyes. Sam had no love handles; he

didn't possess a spare ounce anywhere on his body. Considering she'd added several sizes to her clothing, she found that somewhat annoying. "I'm holding on. Ready anytime you are." She was, and for some reason, she liked it.

"Maybe I should pick Vivi up at the airport tomorrow on this bike. She'd probably enjoy the ride."

Maddie resisted the urge to pinch his nonexistent love handles. "I ordered her a taxi."

"I'll pick her up."

"Perhaps I should go with you."

"That would be great." He gunned the engine, and they took off. Maddie held on to Sam, and a few miles out of the city limits, when she felt comfortable with the leaning of the bike and the feel of holding him, she relaxed.

Sam grinned. His little wife needed to let her hair down more often—with him.

MADDIE WASN'T SURE what she expected from a woman named Vivi who, according to *Wine* magazine, devoured men like bonbons. Maddie and her mother had discussed the situation and decided situating Vivi in Franny and Virgil's house was the best idea. Even though Maddie wanted Sam to go back where he'd been happily living before he found out about their twins, she was bothered by the niggle of jealousy that attacked her every time she thought of the woman's name. *Vivi* seemed so feminine. So sexy. So unlike plain Maddie. Overweight Maddie. She sighed, wishing her heart wasn't such a wussy organ.

She'd set her course, and she would face it

bravely. It was the right thing to do; it was the only thing to do.

Never did she suspect that lovely Vivi would get off the plane and charm her into a semihypnotic trance. The French woman brought adorable toys for the babies and a generous bottle of French perfume for Maddie.

Vivi gushed over the babies, exclaimed over the house and entertained Joey. Maddie had never seen her brother so charmed by someone twice his age. Vivi teased Severn and Virgil, who quite frankly had never seen that much Sophia Loren in French blonde since the days of Marilyn Monroe. Sara and Franny soon lost their suspicion of such a beautiful, sexy woman and pronounced her a delight, particularly when Henry spit up on Vivi's sweater, causing her to shrug and say, "It washes. So much more important that the bubble came out of you, *Henri,* because you are more comfortable now, *oui?*"

But the most remarkable thing was that cool, calm, collected, devoted-to-Sam Martin captured Vivi's heart.

"It's the last thing I expected," Maddie told Sam one night as they sat in the redecorated jungle bedroom. "I thought I would be so jealous of Vivi."

"I never liked Vivi. I told you it was only business for me. Truthfully, she isn't my kind of woman at all."

Maddie liked hearing that. "I wouldn't have thought she was Martin's, either. And it's not just a bonbon thing with her. She was smitten the moment she met Martin. I can't understand it at all. To me,

Martin has always been like a big brother. Except when he's doing your dirty work.''

"Hey! Maddie, Martin is the only person I would have trusted with the personal details of our lives.''

She sniffed. "Have you decided to buy Vivi's company?''

"No. How long is she staying?''

"Until you say you will buy it,'' Maddie told him stubbornly. "It's the only paperwork I ever want Martin to do that concerns the two of us.''

"If I agree, will you do one thing for me?''

Sam's pleading expression sent a tremor through Maddie's heart. How difficult it was to tell him no about anything! "Agree to a custodial arrangement?''

"Kiss me,'' he said.

Her gaze skittered nervously away before returning to his. "That's a high price to pay, isn't it? Considering the circumstances?''

"I would be willing to pay anything you asked for a kiss.''

The tremors turned to an earthquake rocking her heart's core. "Just one kiss? And you'll agree to purchase Jardin?''

"Just one. And I sic Martin on the paperwork.''

It was what she wanted. Sam would return to France. She would raise her sons in peace, with their families for support. He would not be burdened by an obligation she'd forced on him. That was not the way to an equal marriage.

Just a kiss. Lips on lips. Pressure, suction, release. Definitely doable.

Still, she hedged. "I kissed you the other day, remember, when our parents were celebrating the glories of the grape. Can you accept that as a retroactive kiss?''

''I don't think that's acceptable.''

With the babies upstairs with Joey, she really had no reason, no excuse not to. ''Pucker up, huh?''

She puckered, and prayed it would be fast. He was calling the shots, though, since only he knew what kind of kiss he would accept for this agreement. Unable to stand the waiting, since he stood there smiling an enigmatic smile, and she felt pretty silly wearing the type of pucker eating a grapefruit induced, she closed her eyes.

And waited.

She didn't dare open her eyes again, even though she didn't feel him step any closer. The hairs on her arms tingled, and she was pretty certain her antiperspirant quit working.

His hands closed around her upper arms, and her head started swimming. ''Hurry, Sam,'' she whispered.

''No way,'' he told her. ''This kiss is going to last all night.''

''All night!'' Her eyes flew open. ''The babies—''

''I paid Joey to baby-sit for the night. It's time you and I spend some time alone. Together. Wherever that takes us.'' He began kissing a sinuous trail along her neck, sending streaks of pleasure splintering through her body.

''You said one kiss!''

''And I meant that.'' He ran a palm down her back to settle into the small crevice of her spinal curve. ''One long, continuous kiss.''

"Sam!"

"No more, but no less. It was unromantic of me to fall asleep on you the other night. I'm making up for not living up to my boasting."

She shut her eyes tightly again and strangled the moan threatening to escape her throat as she tilted her head back. "I think you're pushing the boundaries of the agreement. This is bribery, I'm positive."

"I know a good lawyer you could ask, but he's busy at the moment with a certain French lady."

Vivi had been staying with Franny and Virgil, as they had a nice guest room. "Is Martin at Mother's with Vivi?"

"They're out on a date, but if you want me to page him—"

"No. That won't be necessary." Her knees were weak under the onslaught of wonderful sensations and remembered passions of other nights. "But I would like to protest the length of the agreed-upon kiss."

"You didn't ask me to specify," he reminded her. "I would have been more than happy to discuss it with you. But doing is more exciting than talking, and I like holding you. I like it a lot."

He's leaving for France, she told herself, as his kiss brushed the cleft between her breasts. *He's leaving for France,* she reminded herself, squeezing her eyes tightly together as he kissed her navel.

Don't go to France! her mind shouted.

She must have said it aloud because he said, "I'm not. I'm staying right here."

Chapter Eight

Maddie tried to jump away from Sam and the soul-on-fire kiss, but he held her tightly as he moved slowly back up toward her lips. "Sam, you have to stop."

"I don't want to. It's wonderful to hold you again."

She put both hands on his chest, pushing slightly. "Sam, you said you'd buy Jardin."

"I am," he said. "Martin's going to France to oversee it for me. He's asking Vivi to marry him tonight. I'm happy this has all worked out so well, because I know you felt like you'd cost me the acquisition." He took her wrists, removing them from his chest so that he could hold her against him instead. "Being with you means more to me than a company, Maddie."

She shakily drew a breath. "You seduce me with words, and you seduce me with kisses. You make me want more." Slight tearing blurred her eyes. "Okay. So you have your own wine company to help you kick-start a major wine-making operation here in Texas. You're happy. But how long do these good feelings last before we get all tangled up again?''

Quickly stripping off her dress, himself of his jeans and shirt, he pulled her over to the bed, folded her under the lace coverlet and settled beside her, holding her in his arms.

''I couldn't be happier about the twins.'' Sam smoothed her hair against his chest, but Maddie couldn't relax.

''Would you want more children?'' This was a worry which ate at her. What if he did?

''Yes, I do. And we'll have them the old-fashioned way.''

''What are the odds?'' She so wanted to believe that they could, but it was the big question mark. And a source of great pain to them previously. It had ripped their marriage apart.

''Same as any other. There's no guarantee Maitland could get you pregnant again, Maddie. Maybe it was luck. Maybe my deposit was potent when you had the procedure, but it had only been in the freezer a few months. By the time you decide to try again, it might be too frozen to thaw for the big swim.''

A tiny smile lifted the corner of her mouth. ''I doubt that.''

''I do know this.'' He ran his fingers through her hair, his touch mesmerizing. ''This issue or any other, I'm not leaving you again.''

''I wish I could believe it would be as simple as you make it sound.'' Maddie sighed. ''I suppose we'd have to try again soon.''

''How soon?''

"Maybe the six-month mark, if we want the best chance for conception."

He turned her to face him. "Is that healthy?"

"I don't know."

"What if it does take? Won't that be hard on your body?"

"Maybe. But I'll be that much closer to forty. I'm racing against time."

"I can be happy with two—"

"I can too. But I want to try. I really do. I'll call in my marker on an all-night-long kiss and much more when it's time."

"And pay for Joey to baby-sit, too?"

Sam was teasing her, and she liked it. She lightly brushed his lips with hers. "I think that's fair enough."

"Can you tell me what night so I'll be prepared?"

She shook her head, her eyes twinkling with mischief. "We agreed we hated making love on a schedule. Therefore, the date of the next all-night kiss is a secret."

"You're always full of surprises. I like that about you, even when they're momentous."

She put her head back on his chest, taking a deeply contented breath. "You're not so bad yourself."

"So is this like a test? A trial and error kind of thing? If we manage to get pregnant, we're okay? And if we can't, we're off again?"

"I don't like the way that sounds," she murmured.

"Neither do I, obviously."

"If we couldn't make it happen together, Sam, I would want to consult with Dr. Maitland again and see if he thought utilizing the same procedure would work. And you've already said no to that option, so I believe that door is firmly shut.''

"And so? It would be over between us? Because we couldn't have more children?''

"This is the same conclusion that ended our marriage,'' she reminded him. ''We're tracking over the same territory. I want children, and you're happy with the picture as it is.''

"Yeah, I should just pack up and leave for France with Vivi and Martin,'' he grumbled.

"You could probably get on the same plane, if you call for a ticket now.''

He shook his head. ''No way. You don't realize how badly you want me.''

That was the stomach-upending, roller coaster part of the problem. She did want Sam badly. He was irresistible. No matter how much she wanted to get over him, no matter how she tried to force her heart not to love him, she did.

She could be happy with him and the twins forever. It was knowing that she and Sam couldn't handle bigger crises than this in their marriage that worried her.

"Sam, I have to tell you something.'' She raised up on her arm and stared down into his face. ''I'm not just being stubborn about having more babies. I know this is going to sound totally postpartum, but I *have* to try again.'' She took a deep breath. ''I have the strangest sensation that someone's missing.''

His eyes widened. ''Someone's…missing?''

"Yes.'' She nodded. ''I know it sounds kind of uncanny, and I wish it didn't. I've tried to put the feeling down to the fact that maybe I'd like a girl, since I've got two boys. Or maybe I had it fixed in my mind that I wanted a big family, so that's what seems 'right' to me. I've tried to convince myself that's all it is.''

He took her hand in his, softly rubbing it. ''But you're not convinced.''

Slowly, she shook her head.

After a moment, he kissed her fingers. ''I'll try as hard as I can to find that elusive youngster, morning, noon and night.'' Grabbing her, he pulled her under him, kissing her thoroughly.

''Sam!'' She beat at his back playfully, trying to throw him off, but he wouldn't go.

''Yes?'' He stopped the kissing long enough to stare down into her eyes.

Maddie felt her breath catch. ''You don't feel it, do you? The missing baby?''

He nuzzled her neck. ''Yes, I most certainly do. You're my missing baby. I'm in the process of locating you right now.'' Swiftly, he ran an exploring hand over her breasts, his eyebrow cocked as if he was searching for something.

''Sam!'' she exclaimed with a laugh.

''The truth is,'' he murmured as he put his face between her breasts, ''you're using this as an excuse. It's the barrier you're putting between us to stay pulled back from me.''

She frowned, but he was paying no attention. Her breasts had his complete focus. Apparently he'd found what he'd been playfully searching for, and what he was doing felt so wonderful that all she could think about was how badly she missed being joined with him. Gently, she tugged him away from her. "Do you really think so?"

His gaze met hers. "Yeah. I do. It's the ultimate dead end, isn't it? The super-goal I probably can't meet."

Her eyes filled with tears. "I'm sorry, Sam. I don't think I saw it that way."

He touched her cheek, running a finger over her skin. "Self-protection is a natural instinct, Maddie. Don't be sad. I better than anyone understand being scared."

"Why?" she whispered.

"Hey, who was in France? Nothing like escaping to a different continent to try to outrun my inadequacy."

She put her fingers in his hair, running them through the dark strands. "Why are you so understanding?"

He laid his head against her chest, and she wrapped her arms around him. "Because I have a beautiful wife I want to keep," he said simply. "If I want to earn her trust back, I know I have to outthink her. She is, after all, determined to send me back to France, even if she has to buy me a wine company."

"Sam!" She pecked at his back with her fingers. "I just didn't want you to give up your dream because of what I did."

"You could have lost your dream because of what *I* did. So I have to figure out how to win my way back into your heart. And I'm not just doing this for you," he told her quite seriously. "I'm setting a good example for my sons."

"They're just babies," she said, her heart swelling with hope at the earnest tone in Sam's voice.

"They're miracles," he told her. "I don't want to lose any of you."

Of course, she wanted to say that he couldn't. But the truth was he had. "Mother says the second time's the charm," she whispered.

"I've very rarely known Franny to be wrong," he muttered, his head back against Maddie's chest as he closed his eyes. "Or my mom. I guess mothers are a special breed. I'll have to make a note of that."

Maddie was pretty sure he fell asleep then. Wiping away a tear, she gently stroked his hair.

Actually, fathers were a very special breed themselves, particularly this one. Her heart heavy, she stared at the ceiling. "Make a note of this, Sam," she whispered. "I'm so afraid of not being the woman you think I am."

She couldn't stop thinking about those papers, which Sam had stuffed away in the kitchen somewhere. He didn't trust her. He said he had to earn her trust back, when the truth was neither of them trusted the other.

Martin and Vivi had fallen in love instantly. They trusted each other with innocent blindness. Newfound love was miraculous that way.

Just like babies.

I miss that innocence.

"Go slow. Go slow," Sam reminded himself as he drove Martin and Vivi to the airport. He wasn't thinking about driving, but about winning Maddie back. The agreement was signed. He owned Jardin.

But he wanted Maddie, who was in the passenger seat beside him and as unattainable as if she were moving to France with his lawyer and the French-woman. Caution, Stop, Heart Veering out of Control were the road signs of his heart. It was a problem.

Problem solving was what successful businessmen were good at, right?

"So, nothing more romantic than getting married in the city of love, eh, Sam?" Martin asked. "Maybe you and Maddie should come over and have a wedding redux after Vivi and I break in the city a little for you."

"Martin," Sam growled. He didn't dare look at Maddie.

"They will come over when they are ready," Vivi said. "I am looking forward to Maddie seeing what she is now the proud part-owner of."

Oops. Sam glanced at Maddie. Her blond brows elevated as she stared at him.

"I'm not a part-owner of Jardin," she said.

Silence spread in the car, a long, drawn-out quiet that Sam spent privately cursing Vivi's effusiveness. "Actually, you are," he told Maddie. "I was going to tell you soon. Myself," he called over his shoulder.

"I am sorry, Sam," Vivi murmured. "I had no idea."

Of course she hadn't. His instructions to keep quiet about the matter had been to Martin.

"I don't understand," Maddie said. Her lips were parted as she stared at him, and he wanted to kiss her, but he told himself he really couldn't in traffic, and certainly not with the audience in the back seat.

"Let me discuss it with you later." He jerked his gaze away from Maddie and thumped the steering wheel. "Bad traffic today."

No one said anything to that. Glancing in the rear-view mirror, he saw Martin sneak a kiss from Vivi. Sam pulled his gaze away, sighing. Who would have ever thought this would have come from Maddie's impromptu invitation? Vivi was clearly smitten, Martin was gaga and Maddie was…cool. "It's hot," Sam grumbled, not because he was, but complaining gave him a chance to vent. He reached over and flipped the air conditioner up a notch.

Maddie caught his wrist in midair, forcing him to meet her gaze as they sat stranded at the stoplight. The question in her eyes was obvious. "Wouldn't be any fun to own a winery without you," he muttered under his breath. "You're the one who made it possible. We're in it together. But let's talk about it when we're alone."

"We were very alone last night, but you didn't tell me."

"We were playing detective."

She frowned. "You had plenty of time to tell me."

"Yeah, well. I was enjoying searching through the lost-and-found."

She had a shiver just thinking about how thoroughly Sam had kissed her. Of course, he hadn't paid a bit of attention to what she'd told him.

"Did you?" he asked softly.

"What?" She snapped out of her longing reverie.

"Find anything you'd lost?" he asked under his breath.

They were hunting, but not finding much. And she

couldn't take it lightly. "Trust is hard to find again. I think you should have discussed your decision with me."

Vivi and Martin were exchanging love talk and obviously weren't tuned in to her and Sam anymore, so Maddie released Sam's hand and stared out the opposite window.

"I wanted it to be a surprise," he told her.

"It is that." She wondered why being part-owner of Jardin made her uncomfortable.

Maybe Sam's right. He's trying to share his life with me, and I'm too scared to do the same.

"Here we are at the airport," he said.

The sound of a motorcycle roaring up alongside them made everybody turn. Joey tapped on Maddie's window.

"Joey!" she exclaimed, letting her window down. "What are you doing here?"

"Our folks took Henry to the hospital. He had a high fever and was sick to his stomach for so long they decided he better go."

Henry, the baby who never wanted to eat.

"Oh, no!" She jumped out of the car, instantly reaching for the helmet Joey handed her.

Somehow, she remembered to wave goodbye to Vivi and Martin. Her fingers clenched Joey's sides as the motorcycle roared away from the curb, and she thought she heard Sam's voice call something to her, but her heart was frozen with fear for her baby and she couldn't think.

She just hung on.

Sam pulled up beside them at the exit booth.

"Come on," he said to Maddie. "We do this together."

SAM COULDN'T HELP thinking as he stared through the nursery window at his tiny son that the tubes sticking into him had to be painful.

Emergency surgery for an underdeveloped small intestine. Sam closed his eyes, running the same thought through his mind over and over. *Please let him be all right. Please let him be all right.*

Maddie touched his arm. "Sam?"

Opening his eyes, he stared at the unmoving infant. "Yes?"

"Are you okay?"

Why couldn't he look at her? The pain stayed inside him, in a place where only he could examine it. He didn't answer for a moment. The little arms and legs in the clear plastic bassinet held his entire attention.

"Sam?" Maddie asked again. "You said we'd do this together," she murmured.

That was before, when he thought he had everything to gain and nothing else to lose. Henry was so soft and defenseless. How could he not protect his son? They wouldn't even let him in to see him very often. When Sam did go in, it was all he could do not to cry.

Maddie cried. She had the pediatric nurse, Katie Topper, comforting her, and Dr. Abby. Dr. Mitchell Maitland stopped by every once in a while to check on her.

Sam opted for the strong, silent demeanor while everyone comforted his wife. He let them comfort her, so he could keep from crying himself. *My poor son. I thought all I had to do was come back to Texas and everyone would live happily ever after.* "I can't stand the thought of losing him," he whispered.

Maddie leaned her head against his shoulder. "Oh, Sam."

"Twins seemed like one too many at first. Now I know that losing one would be…losing too much."

Maddie didn't say anything to that, but she squeezed his arm. He was probably making her sad, but he didn't mean to. The tiny head in the bassinet moved slightly, and Sam willed his strength to his son. *Fight, Henry. Fight.*

"I'M WORRIED ABOUT SAM," Maddie told Franny and Sara. "All he does is stand and look in that window."

She could hardly bear the heartbroken look on her handsome husband's face. His remoteness frightened her. "I've never known him to keep everything locked inside like this."

Sara shook her head. "He's always tended to get quiet when he's upset."

"He's worried about his son," Franny said, her tone thoughtful. "Nothing like worrying about a child to really take the taste out of your grits."

Sam had been quiet when they'd separated too. Courteous, formal, quiet. Then he'd left for France and she'd never heard from him again.

Maddie wrapped her arms around herself. The feeling of aloneness was startling.

If she was feeling it this badly, Sam was, too. She

went to stand beside him again. "Sam," she whispered.

"Yes?"

He might as well have been speaking to someone he didn't know. "Sam, you weren't here when the babies were born, but they looked an awful lot like this."

There was no answer. Maddie thought maybe she'd found the right approach.

"They had tubes then, too, which were always hard for me to look at. Even though they supposedly were healthy and weighed a normal amount for twins, I was scared to death. They appeared weak and helpless, a lot like Henry does now."

Sam shook his head. Then he wiped at his cheek. Maddie silently put her hand in her husband's and didn't say another word.

"I DON'T THINK THIS IS going so well," Franny confided to Sara. "Sam doesn't say a word to Maddie. He's like a giant block of granite that never moves from that spot."

"He's going to make himself ill," Sara concurred. "Both Severn and I have tried to talk to him, but I'm beginning to wonder if he's in shock."

"Two days is a long time to go incommunicado." Franny frowned. "Maddie is beside herself. Not only does she worry about Henry, she's worried about Sam. Frankly, I'm worried about her."

"This can't be healthy for either one of them."

Franny heard the distress in Sara's voice. She took her friend's hand in her own, patting it. They clung to each other for a moment, seeking strength.

"A marriage is built on sharing. Shared strength, shared happiness, shared sadness," Sara said. "But you can't make two people turn to each other."

"I think you're right," Franny agreed sadly. "I wish we could help somehow, but this is something Maddie and Sam are going to have to work out between themselves."

Sara nodded. "The funny thing is, I have a feeling Henry is going to be just fine. It's Maddie and Sam who are in need of healing right now." She sighed unhappily. "I had such high hopes, Franny. I just knew that this time they'd work it all out."

"Second time's the charm," Franny said softly. "I hoped it was, anyway."

"It's terrible to have to stand by and watch your child suffer. Sam and Maddie are watching Henry, and we're watching Sam and Maddie."

Franny shook her head. Sam might as well have been back in France, because he sure wasn't where anyone could reach him.

Not even Maddie.

Chapter Nine

One week later, Maddie had to face the fact that everything she and Sam had argued about had been trivial. Nothing mattered except having a happy, healthy family.

Henry was back home, eating more normally than he had.

But Sam had moved next door with his parents. He slept on the couch during the day, coming over at night to sit up with the babies. Maddie was getting a lot of rest, but her heart was shattered.

He barely spoke to anyone. It was as if he'd appointed himself the guardian of her and the children, a quiet protector of the night.

It was week four in the twins' lives—and ground zero in her marriage.

And that's when she knew she'd harbored a dream that, this time, Sam wanted her enough to stick out the good times and the bad. The pain and the pleasure.

It broke her heart.

"Have you tried talking to him?" Franny asked her daughter.

"Yes." Sam had ceased communicating the moment he saw his tiny son with needles in him, out of the reach of Sam's sheltering arms. "I've even tried not talking to him, so he could have some space."

Franny scratched her mop of iron-gray, scattered curls. "The man is suffering."

"I know." Maddie put some baby clothes in the washer. "Sometimes when I wake up in the night, I can hear him pacing overhead in the nursery. I think he just stands there and stares at those babies. Like maybe he's afraid they're going to stop breathing or something."

"I can understand that." Franny reached for some miniature baby booties, matching them expertly and rolling them into pairs. "To receive something you wanted desperately, when you didn't even know it was possible, is a miracle. To have it snatched away almost as unexpectedly would be very traumatic."

Maddie set down the detergent. "I never thought of it that way."

"I didn't, either, until you mentioned he paces the floor at night." Franny shrugged. "His sons are awfully delicate, Maddie, if you think about it. Sam's had no experience with younger siblings, or babies in general. He doesn't know that the twins look just like other babies. I'll bet he is worried out of his skull over them."

Maddie's heart lightened at the possible explanation. "You could be right."

"And if you consider the fact that he might think what happened to Henry was the result of something he did wrong, and he didn't know it, wouldn't that make it all the more upsetting?" She folded some diapers in two, and reached for receiving blankets. "It wasn't like he could say, 'oh, we've been feeding this baby wrong,' or 'I didn't do this right, so I'll have to be more careful in the future.' He couldn't see what was wrong with the baby nor can he take any precautions that something like that doesn't happen again."

"It's out of his control."

"Right."

Maddie nodded. "I suppose that makes sense. But," she said, drawing a deep breath, "I had this idea that we would work through problems together."

Franny clasped her weathered hands. "Maybe that's asking too much of any marriage sometimes. Perhaps that's putting Sam up on some high pedestal, in a position where he can't live up to your expectations."

"Do you think so?" Maddie stared at her mother, who shrugged.

"Everyone grieves and worries and celebrates differently, I'd say. Sam's frozen right now. He's in pain. I don't think he meant to shut you out, but I reckon this time maybe it's better to just understand that he's coping the best he can."

"You're right. I've been thinking of myself."

"No." Franny touched her daughter's hair with loving fingers. "You spend more time thinking about him than you realize. And your babies. Sometimes we just have to rethink matters, and then the answer comes out differently."

Maddie smiled and took her mother's hand. "Thanks, Mom."

Franny squeezed her fingers. "Your turn is coming one day, my dear. Mothers spend a lot of time thinking about their children. But then they're older, and suddenly, a bandage on the knee just isn't the answer anymore."

"I love you, Mom."

"It's all going to work out fine." Franny smiled. "You're a lovely daughter, and my son-in-law is a good man. A mother couldn't hope for more than that."

THAT NIGHT, when Sam's pacing began, Maddie put on a cotton bathrobe that reached her knees. She warmed up some tea in the kitchen and took it upstairs. Without saying a word, she set it on a coffee table, then squeezed his arm as he stared down at the wrapped bundles in the baby cribs. He didn't respond.

She went back downstairs to bed.

The next night when the pacing began, she did the same thing. This time, Sam patted her hand when she touched his arm. He didn't say anything, and neither did Maddie. After a moment, she went back to bed.

When she awakened the next morning, he was gone, of course, and the grandmothers were upstairs in the nursery. "Good morning," Maddie said. "I'm beginning to feel like a princess."

"You won't believe this," Sara told her with shining eyes, "but this morning when we arrived, Sam was fast asleep on the couch!"

That was a good sign. "I didn't drug his tea, I promise."

Franny swiftly diapered Hayden. "Sam's going to come around. We just have to be patient with the man."

Sara sat down in a rocker with Henry. "I appreciate you being so patient with my son, Franny. To tell you the truth, I was starting to get a bit embarrassed."

"No need," Franny said. "Family pulls together." She met her daughter's eyes, and Maddie nodded.

It wasn't the way Maddie had pictured it, but pulling together was so much better than pulling apart. Sam was afraid for his children, and needed to be reassured. He wanted an eye kept on them twenty-four hours a day.

There was a way both goals—reassuring Sam and monitoring the babies—could be accomplished. "I've got an idea," she suddenly said. "If you think the grandfathers wouldn't mind running an errand for me."

SAM STARED AT the new camera monitor in the nursery. It wasn't like any he had ever seen. This was more than an audio monitor.

There was a note attached. "To Daddy, Love, Henry and Hayden," he read. But the words were written in Maddie's delicate hand. He sighed, deeply touched that she would give him a gift in the babies' names.

He knew he'd neglected his wife. That was the last thing he wanted. All through his silence, when he couldn't move, could barely think, he'd been aware of her gentle, caring presence.

It was as if she understood he could only concentrate on the overwhelming fear and panic over his ill child. As if she knew he had to make his own way back.

He tucked a blanket around each infant carefully, felt each small forehead, before brushing a kiss there. The babies felt warm, alive.

Nodding, he felt the thunder in his heart quiet down to a mere echo. His children were going to be fine.

Going downstairs, he looked in the kitchen for the other end of the monitor his sons had given him. Not really sure what he was looking for, he meandered into his old study, finding no new gadget there. Reluctantly, he went into the bedroom he'd once shared with Maddie.

She was sound asleep, her shoulders visible above the sheet, her shiny brown hair streaming across the white pillowcase. He swallowed, scanning the room.

There, next to the bed, was a white, mushroom-shaped stand with a screen. He leaned closer, seeing Henry and Hayden resting in their cribs. For several moments, he stood watching his sons, his heart beginning to pound again. When they didn't move, but remained sleeping as peacefully as his wife, he turned his attention back to Maddie.

She nestled beneath the covers, undisturbed. Fierce possessiveness took hold of Sam. *I miss sleeping with her.*

But the monitor was his gift, wasn't it? And she'd put it in her room, so…could that possibly be an invitation? He didn't dare hope.

Still, it could be construed as an invitation. A man

couldn't be blamed for making himself comfortable where he could enjoy his sons' gift, could he?

He wanted to be with Maddie. Stripping off his jeans and shirt, he carefully crawled into bed beside her. She curled up into his shoulder, just like in the old days, and Sam smiled.

SAM AND MADDIE DIDN'T awaken until they heard the voices.

"I think I'm breaking out in hives from the uncertainty!" Sara said. "I don't want to rush matters, but I thought those two would be able to work something out by now. I'm beginning to worry." She leaned over to pick up an infant from its crib in the nursery.

"They're like two horses in the same halter that can't get their gait in the right rhythm," Franny agreed. "Virgil and I have decided that if Sam's going to be here for good, we'd like to head back to our farm. It hasn't sold yet, and frankly, we miss the quiet of the country, and working the cotton fields. But we can't go, not while there's so much turmoil in the family."

"I know." Sara sighed, the sound coming over the monitor clearly. "I'm worried about Severn. He's happy holding the babies, and I think he still wants to buy the house next door, but he's also itching to take a cruise. Once he retired, he thought he'd do everything he couldn't do when he was working. He may have caught some globe-hopping fever from Sammy. Of course, we've never been out of the country at all. But I'll tell you a secret," she whispered.

Maddie and Sam sat up in bed, their faces closer to the monitor.

"We got our passports made!"

Franny giggled girlishly. "You must never tell Maddie, but we got ours made right before she told us she'd gotten pregnant by that newfangled doctor!" She clapped a hand over her mouth. "That didn't come out right, but you know what I mean. Gracious! I'll have to watch how I talk around anyone but you, Sara! All of our friends think Maddie got pregnant before Sam left for France." She nodded, satisfied. "And we never saw the need to disabuse them of the notion. Why, these two pumpkins are too pretty to have come out of test tubes!"

She cooed to the baby in her arms, tracing its cheek with a grandmotherly finger.

Sara shook her head. "Virgil and I haven't done much traveling ourselves, of course. Maybe if things settle down here between Maddie and Sam, the four of us could take a cruise together. Wouldn't that be nice?"

The grandmothers settled into two rockers in range of the camera, each cuddling a freshly diapered infant.

Maddie and Sam glanced at each other in dismay.

"We should turn the monitor off. It's like we're spying on our own mothers!" Maddie whispered, even though the sound wouldn't transmit in the opposite direction. She shivered. "When you were young, did your mother ever tell you she had eyes in the back of her head and knew everything you were doing?"

"No," he whispered back. "She said she knew

me like the back of her hand and knew everything I was going to do *before* I did it.''

''That's even worse! I'm shutting this thing off.'' Maddie leaned over him to switch off the monitor she'd placed beside the bed, but Sam stopped her.

''What if they're doing it on purpose?''

Maddie frowned. Sam wasn't wearing a shirt. He'd worn boxers to bed, but everything else was gloriously revealed for viewing. ''When did you get in bed with me?''

He shrugged large, powerful shoulders. ''After I found my present from my sons.''

She glanced back at the screen. The mothers were still chatting away, but it no longer seemed like a good idea to have the monitor so nearby. ''Some gift that turned out to be. I feel like a bad P.I.''

''We're probably raising little spies. And I bet they get a healthy dose of that gene from their grandmothers.''

''Do you really think they're setting us up? Pretending they don't know we're listening?''

''I don't know. But our mothers wouldn't be above invoking a guilt trip.''

''Hmm.'' Maddie forced her focus away from Sam in her bed and onto the monitor. ''Scheming is something they've stooped to on the odd occasion.''

''On the oft occasion.''

''Okay.'' She mulled over that for a second. ''Does your father really want to take a cruise, to travel out of the country?''

''My father gets seasick in a swimming pool. Moving to Austin to live next door to you was the first relocation in their entire marriage. Mom used to

complain because Dad never wanted to vacation anywhere that didn't start with *T-E-X-A-S*."

"Oh." Maddie turned her attention back to Sam.
"I remember Dad saying that if he never had to look
through cotton leaves for weevils again, it would be
too soon. And that he was tired of being away from
Mom twelve hours or more a day." Her eyes were
huge. "But they never mentioned that they'd gotten
their passports. I didn't know they'd thought about
traveling. They stayed here because of me, Sam. I
feel like I've taken their retirement dreams from
them."

"Don't feel too guilty just yet." Sam eyed Maddie
thoughtfully. "My guess is it's a setup. Maybe we
should react appropriately."

"What do you want to do?"

They both glanced back at the monitor.

"I'd better go wake Maddie up," Franny said. "I
don't think these little tykes are going to wait much
longer to eat."

"I'm grateful Sam felt like he could leave these
babies to be monitored. I'm sure he enjoyed a good
night's rest, even if he does sleep on my old sofa."

"At least he's sleeping now," Franny said cheerfully. "I wasn't sure how much longer he could go
on staying awake all night. Maddie had a true brain-
storm about the monitor."

"It sure seems to have given Sam peace of mind."
Sara moved close to the monitor, peering at the
screen. "Wonder how this gadget works, anyway?"

Maddie and Sam both instinctively pulled the
sheet up on their bodies, even though they couldn't
be seen.

"I don't know. Something to do with the babies' heartbeats or something. Like the one they had in the hospital, I guess. With Virgil and Severn putting it together, the silly thing probably doesn't work at all. Maybe the effect on Sam is really like one of those placebo things. It doesn't really work, but his mind thinks it does." She giggled, and Sara laughed with her, her face still looming in the monitor screen.

Sam and Maddie leaned back in the bed.

"I'll be right back," Franny said as she left the room. Sara stared a moment more into the screen, perplexed, before moving away.

Maddie stared at Sam, stricken. "We have to do something. They're not going to rest until they believe our marriage is going to work out."

"I don't know if we can work anything out if they're going to devote their lives to trying to fix ours. I know they mean well but..."

They looked at each other for a moment.

"'A serene environment should be encouraged, where we can enjoy optimum new parenthood.' I'm quoting your mom and mine. This is pressure, Sam!" Maddie glanced down at the sheet still clutched between them. "But what if they're not setting us up? What if we really are keeping them from what they want to do in life? That's a horrible thing to do to our parents!"

"There's only one way to find out what they're really up to," Sam said. "Hold still."

Chapter Ten

"What are you doing?" Maddie asked with a squeal, as Sam's warm and well-built body suddenly covered her, pressing her to the bed in a manner most familiar and somehow welcome.

"Calling their bluff."

Good idea. No, bad, bad idea! Maddie thought as Sam's lips claimed hers. Bad because memories of sweet lovemaking washed over her, of shared happiness it hurt to remember.

Good because she missed Sam so much, missed their marriage so much, that she wished they'd never separated.

And then bad again, because she knew that what was broken could never be fixed. It could never be whole and innocent with wonder the way it had been.

Sam stared down into her eyes. "You're beautiful," he said huskily, before closing his mouth over hers again just as Franny opened the door.

They heard a gasp, and then the door closing, with a slow and cautious effort not to let them know they'd been seen.

But Sam didn't stop kissing her. Maddie shut her

eyes. Just a trifle guiltily, she ran her hands from his shoulders to his waist, feeling the weight and firm skin of her husband.

"She's gone," she whispered.

"I don't want to stop," he replied against her lips, his voice low.

"If we don't, it might not be our mothers' bluff that gets called."

He pulled back to stare into her eyes. "It would be so much easier," he said with a sigh, "if putting our marriage back together could be based on our sexual compatibility."

"I know." A warm smile lit her face. "It's like trying to fight with both arms tied behind your back, isn't it?"

"And a broken ankle. I get close to you, and all I can think about is how I felt when we made love."

A shriek interrupted Maddie's reply. Maddie and Sam jolted upright and stared at the monitor screen.

"They're in bed! They're in bed!" Franny yelped to Sara.

Sara turned from adjusting the infant she held. "Of course. Just tell Maddie it's time to feed the babies."

"They're in bed together!"

Sara gasped. "You're kidding!"

Both mothers bent to peer at the camera. Sam and Maddie shrank back.

Franny banged on the monitor, sending nerve-jangling thumps into the bedroom. "This thing doesn't work worth a tinker's damn! It could have warned us Sam was in bed with Maddie. I'm going to tell Virgil to take it back to the store."

The picture went out a second later.

"They weren't setting us up, Sam," Maddie said. "They really would like to get on with their lives." She looked at him sadly. "I know I said I didn't want to have a pseudoromance with you, but I suppose it would be best if they could feel satisfied that everything is fine between us."

Sam got out of bed. "I can fake it if you can."

"Fake it?" For some reason, her heart stung a little at his choice of words.

"Fake that everything's going to be just fine."

"Oh." *Won't it?* she wanted to ask. Of course, she'd done everything she could to push Sam away. Maybe it was like hearing her mother and Sara talk when they thought no one was listening. Sam had been telling her all along what he thought she wanted to hear.

He would do that. It would never cross Sam's mind not to take care of his children, and thus, a wife he was married to in name only.

"So? Are we faking it?" he asked. "So they can get on with their lives?"

She nodded slowly. "I'm faux if you are. There's a French word for you," she said, trying to make her smile bright.

"Great. Let's go feed those boys." He snapped off the monitor.

"Okay." But Maddie's heart felt strange, like it somehow wasn't hers anymore.

Guess it was my bluff that got called.

SAM THOUGHT IT WAS a great idea to ease the family members' collective minds. It appeared that his parents and in-laws all wanted to be off living their own lives.

And if they were gone, it meant he'd have his wife to himself. For just an instant, when they'd kissed, she'd relaxed against him, her body warm and trusting beneath his. "That's a very big goal," he murmured to himself, watching Maddie carry a baby into the bathroom for a nice warm bath. *I'd like to be alone with my wife so we can work on our marriage without assistance, no matter how well-meaning it may be.*

He carried the other baby in, holding him against his chest as he stood at the side of the tub. Maddie had placed a very small, infant-size tub inside the larger one. She filled it with tepid water, which she tested with her elbow.

"Just right," she told Henry with satisfaction. "In you go, sweetheart."

With gentle hands, she lowered the baby into the water until he was half-submerged. Henry stared up at his mom, his new, curious eyes never leaving hers as he learned trust at her fingertips.

A sweetness went through Sam's very soul as he watched this moment between mother and child.

Love grew with trust. Trust was the soil in which love learned to grow, and walk, and run, and one day, find independence. Henry splashed unexpectedly, a tiny flailing of his arms, and Maddie praised him as she ran a soft cloth gently over his body.

Sam drew a deep breath and wished he and Maddie could learn to trust each other again.

"THERE." Maddie stood, pleased that both her babies were freshly cleaned and wrapped securely in towels against Sam's broad chest. "Oh, that's such a cute picture! Hold on. Let me find the camera."

Sam's shirt was fairly wet. He was out of sorts since he and Maddie had decided to "fake it." Posing right now didn't sit well with him. "I don't want my picture taken."

She paused for just a moment before rooting through a cabinet in the armoire. He followed her out into the bedroom.

"Don't be shy," she teased. "There's nothing sexier than a father holding his children. I want about a hundred pictures like this."

He blinked. Sexy was not how he felt. The descriptive phrase would be "under siege." His heart was being pulled and twisted from every side, and he wasn't good at smiling fake smiles, saying fake words or faking his marriage.

She pulled out the camera, holding it to her eye. He could see her smile beneath the apparatus, her teeth white and even. Taking this picture made her happy. "I don't feel like smiling," he grumbled.

"Think about packing our parents off for their retirement, and the two of us being alone," she suggested.

He grinned.

She snapped the picture.

"That was wonderful! This is going to be a great picture!" She beamed at him. "Thanks, Sam."

Turning away, she flipped the camera over, the whirring sound holding her complete attention.

"Was that the last picture?"

"Yes. I took all the others in the last week of my pregnancy, and then at the hospital."

His eyes widened. "Maddie, I never saw you pregnant."

She glanced up. "That's okay. You didn't miss anything."

Gently, he set the babies down in their matching bassinets. "Yes, I did." He advanced on her as she began tucking the camera back into the drawer.

"I assure you that you did not." She slammed the drawer.

He pulled it open. "We're going to the one-hour photo developer."

"We most certainly are not!"

Reaching around her into the drawer for the camera, he noticed she kept her hands tightly closed. He pretended to root around in the drawer with one hand, all the while keeping her pinned against the armoire, his eyes on hers. After a moment, knowing full well she'd taken the film roll from the camera, he ran his other hand up her side, tickling her. She jumped, but he had her trapped with his body.

"Fair is fair," he told her, using both hands to tickle her now. She twitched and jumped, pushing at him and laughing at the same time. "I know all your most vulnerable spots," he warned.

"Sam!" she squealed. "Stop!"

She couldn't tickle him effectively because she wouldn't let go of the film. He took advantage of this by pressing closer against her. She wiggled to free herself.

Suddenly, she stopped. He stared down at her, watching carefully for her next move.

"Sam," she said, "I know all your vulnerable spots, too."

He crooked a brow at her. "If that's supposed to be a threat, I have to tell you, it sounds remarkably like a promise I'd like you to deliver on."

Her mouth twisted wryly. She slipped her fingers behind his neck, caressing the skin lightly, touching the nape with featherlight strokes.

He shivered, relaxing instantly under her ministrations. "You *will* give me the film," he warned huskily, letting her hypnotize him. "That feels so good. I always loved you scratching my neck."

She smiled, pushing her fingers farther up his nape, massaging below his hair. "Make you sleepy?"

"Not sleepy enough to impair my driving to the Photo Shack." He caught her wrist in his hand, arresting it against his shoulder. "Maddie, I missed it all."

The teasing light fled from her eyes. "I was not a beautiful pregnant woman, Sam."

"I missed it, though. I'm behind the eight ball, Maddie. It's time I can't replace. And Henry getting sick made me realize that I haven't taken in the full miracle of what you did."

Her eyes grew wide. "It was Maitland's miracle."

He shook his head. "No. It was yours. And I can't even begin to understand what your life was like for the last nine months. You'll never know how much I regret that."

She stared at him, her lips parted sweetly.

"How can I fix something that broke if I don't know what it's made of?" he asked. There was a huge gap in their lives. His wife had changed. They had grown apart.

Losing time was a terrifyingly empty feeling.

She put her hand in his. "Come on, Sammy," she said softly. "Drive me to the Photo Shack."

THE FIVE FAMILY MEMBERS stared as Sam and Maddie borrowed Joey's motorcycle and roared off. They waved cheerily and then vroom! off they went like free-spirited soul mates.

Which they were, but unfortunately they hadn't figured that out yet. "I wonder why that's becoming Maddie's favorite mode of travel," Franny murmured. "It isn't seemly for a new mother to be riding a motorcycle, is it?"

Sara shrugged. "I think they find it relaxing. Their hair blows in the wind, they're in tune with the aura of the earth—"

"No way," Joey interrupted. "They're *together.* Maddie's hanging on to Sam, and Sam's got her pressed up against his back. They can be the way they really want to be, under the ruse of running an errand. You know the expression, free to be you and me."

All the parents looked at each other in surprise. Franny gave her a son a narrow look. "You're supposed to be studying and playing football at college. I'm beginning to wonder what you're majoring in."

He grinned. "I'm beginning to wonder how you and Dad made me and Maddie."

They all raised their brows at him.

Laughing, Joey raised a hand. "No, I've got the

birds and the bees figured out, no thanks to the little stick-figure book you gave me.''

Virgil cleared his throat. "Wasn't sure how much you wanted to know, Son. Seemed like all you wanted to do at the time was play catch.''

Joey smiled at his dad. "And all the hours you spent playing catch with me is a major reason why I'm on a football team today, Dad. But it's the time we had together that made me what I am. Sam and Maddie need time together.''

Franny glanced in the direction the motorcycle had gone. "I wish they'd go away on a vacation together, but I know Maddie wouldn't leave the babies that long." She gave a long-suffering sigh. "Come on over to our house, everybody. Virgil and I will serve you some lemonade and cookies while we ruminate on this another moment and hold these young 'uns. There has to be a way for those two to have time alone together!''

"IT'S SNEAKY," Maddie said with a smile. "But I think you may have solved the problem brilliantly.'' The travel agent's office was next door to the photo shack. Sam had surprised her by pulling her inside.

Sam patted his pockets, where the airplane tickets and itinerary lay. "France is beautiful at this time of year.''

She winked at him before putting on the helmet. "I didn't know you could be so crafty. I rather like this side of you.''

"Anything to romance my wife.'' He grinned.

"I don't feel guilty about this when I think of it

as a reverse honeymoon. Only we're not the ones going away.''

He got on the bike. ''If this works, no one will be happier than me.''

She wrapped her arms around his waist as she slid onto the motorcycle behind him.

''I'm going to talk Joey into leaving me the key to his bike while he's gone, too.'' Sam settled himself as snugly as he could between her legs. The feel of his wife molded against him was reason enough for him to purchase a motorcycle this very afternoon.

However, maybe the plane tickets were the best way to get close to his wife to his heart's content— without having to fake it.

And then, with any luck, back into her trust.

''YOU'RE SENDING *US* to France, Sam?''

Sara glanced around the table on Franny and Virgil's porch. Franny could tell Sara and Severn's shock was genuine. As for herself, she felt as if the lemonade had just turned sour in her stomach.

''It would be very helpful to me if you could go,'' Sam said, his expression genuinely concerned. ''Martin's so busy honeymooning with Vivi, I think it'd be best if I had family over there looking after the business for a week.''

Franny turned to her daughter for confirmation, but Maddie's eyes were innocent of intrigue. And Franny knew Maddie didn't have a conspiring bone in her body. She and Sam were acting like such lovebirds Franny was momentarily thrown off.

''It would help us if we knew the family business was in the best of hands,'' Maddie confirmed.

Franny heard the emphasis on "family business" and perked up. "Well, when you put it that way... but we were of the mind that you two were the ones who need a trip. Especially since we're here to baby-sit."

"I can't leave the babies right now, Mom," Maddie said gently. "We'll let you keep them when the time is right for us to go. But Sam's hoping you'll do this for him, so we can stay here and bond with our children."

This was more plea than Franny or Sara could stand. They glanced at their husbands, who seemed somehow caught by the idea.

Joey clapped his hands. "You're springing for my ticket, too?"

"Oh, we can't let Sam do that," Franny demurred. "We'll buy our own tickets."

"Absolutely not. This is a company-paid trip," Sam insisted. "Think of it as my thanks for looking after Maddie when I should have been here doing it myself."

"Oh, you didn't know, Son," Virgil said to his son-in-law. "Our daughter's right ornery about doing things her own way."

Sam nodded. "I agree with you. And that's why I'm doing this my way. I'm staying with her, and sending you five on the business trip this time."

The four parents took each other's measure steadily.

"Sure would like to see the land of grapes," Virgil said.

"Wouldn't mind spending a little of Virgil's money in the stores," Franny said.

"We've always said we wanted to travel," Sara said, pleading with her husband.

Severn shrugged. "No place better to travel than France, I guess. I wouldn't mind expanding my waistline with some French food."

"Yes!" Joey punched the air. "Maybe I'll meet a French gal!"

"Your job is to chaperon them," Sam said, mock-sternly. "I want you to chauffeur them, and get them through customs, and keep a general eye on them."

"There's no telling what they might get into in France," Maddie told her brother. "Actually, I'm not sure you're any more trustworthy than they are. But I'm counting on you to be the level head in the bunch. No falling asleep under patio umbrellas while they snooze off where anyone could steal their money or whatever."

"You make us sound helpless," Franny said. "We've got our orders. We're going to take good care of the family business!"

Maddie and Sam smiled at each other.

"Excellent," Sam said. "And I'll take good care of Maddie."

Chapter Eleven

"Martin," Sam said over the phone the next day, "remember all those times you told me how loyal you were, and how you owed me?"

"This is starting to sound smarmier than I'm used to from my one and only honest client, but, yeah."

Sam grinned at the suspicion in his lawyer's tone. "I'm sending all the family over to France. Consider it an extended wedding gift for you and Vivi."

"The…entire family?" Martin asked carefully.

"Mom, Dad, Franny and Virgil, and Joey. Joey's pretty cool and will help keep the adults out of trouble. I have them staying in a nice hotel in the center of Paris. But if you wouldn't mind—"

"Trying to get some time alone with your wife, Sam?"

"Exactly. We love our family, but we want a little less help in certain departments. And they've been wanting a vacation. Who better than my old buddy Martin to assist all of us in our common goals?"

"Who better, indeed?" Martin sighed. "You should be enjoying a honeymoon over here with Maddie."

"This is the way Maddie and I want it. We want to be with the babies. We want to be with each other. Basically, we want to find our marriage again. To do that, we decided we just want a few days without any…well-meaning assistance."

"I'm your man," Martin said. "What do you want them to do?"

"They think they're coming over to keep an eye on the family business."

"Oh, boy. Vivi's going to love that. She and her brother, Jean-Luc, guard that place like a holy shrine."

Sam grinned. "Vivi wanted American buyers for her wine company. There's a cloud attached to every silver lining."

"I'll tell her you're sending five clouds our way."

"Thanks, Martin."

"Next time, I want it to be you and Maddie who are coming to visit."

"First things first. I've got to convince Maddie that no matter whatever else happens, the four of us were meant to be a family."

"Courtesy of Maitland Maternity."

"Damn right," Sam said. "As far as I'm concerned, giving us twins wasn't the only miracle Dr. Maitland performed. She gave me a chance to get my wife back, Martin. I intend to spend the next week showing Maddie how much I need these particular miracles."

"And then? If she still thinks she wants to be *trois* instead of *quatre?*"

"You keep our parents busy," Sam stated, "and

I'll do my darnedest to go from live-in ex to real husband and father of *deux*."

"That *will* be a miracle," Martin said.

SAM AND MADDIE TOOK their parents and Joey to the airport and saw them off with waves and smiles, and kisses from the grandparents to the grandbabies. The travelers looked dapper, each holding a tiny American flag Maddie had given them and carrying a new picture of the babies in their wallets. Severn and Sara were fashionably attired in navy suits just right for travel. Sara's blouse was red, and Severn's shirt was white. Their elegantly silver hair was combed to perfection.

Franny and Virgil wore comfortable matched red, white and blue windsuits. Franny's iron-colored tufted curls were a bit askew as always, and Virgil stood slightly bent, his face sun-wrinkled and his bald spot red among the pewter strands from all the years on the tractor.

Deep happiness flooded Maddie. They were doing the right thing for their parents, even if they had resorted to some devious tactics in order to send them away for a week.

"I feel like I shouldn't go," Franny wailed. "I'm a traitor to my grandchildren!"

"You should go, Mom," Maddie said somewhat desperately, in case her mother should turn around and march back toward the car. "You and Dad deserve a vacation."

She could see the indecision in her mother's eyes. "You'll be all right, I know," Franny said finally. "Sam will take good care of you." She glanced at her son-in-law. "Please make her rest," she pleaded. "Maddie's such a go-go girl."

"So's her mother." Sam kissed her cheek fondly. "Enjoy yourself. Martin and Vivi will show you all the highlights."

"We'll make sure everything is working smooth as a ribbon at Jardin," she promised Sam.

Virgil shook Sam's hand and kissed his daughter on the cheek. "Bon voyage, I guess. I've always wanted to say that." He grinned sheepishly.

"Have a good time, Dad." Maddie patted her father's cheek as he bent to kiss the babies. "Keep Mom out of trouble."

"Impossible. She does whatever gets set in that gray-haired head of hers." But he took hold of his wife's hand and led her down the gate toward the plane.

Sara and Severn said less painful goodbyes. They kissed everyone again, the babies twice, and hurried after the others.

Joey lingered. "I know what you two are up to."

Sam and Maddie exchanged guilty glances.

"Can't say I blame you for wanting a little time alone together," he said with a sigh. "I know sex would be on my mind if I had the chance."

He ambled down the hall after kissing the babies on their foreheads.

Maddie looked at Sam, her face burning. "Sex isn't on my list," she assured him.

It looked like he made a conscious effort to shake his head. "Nor mine." But a blush spread up his throat.

They stood silently for a moment, looking at each other.

Sam scratched at his neck. "Just out of curiosity, how much longer, anyway?"

"I have my final checkup this week," Maddie said, equally nonchalant. "By my calculations, the night before our folks return, we should be..."

His brows rose. "Good for an all-night kiss?"

She glanced at the baby he held in his arms. "And then some, if you're up to it."

"Oh, I'll be up to it. You can stake our wine company on it."

"This won't be like the last time you thought you'd be up to an all-night kiss?" she asked, eyeing him mischievously. "And ended up sleeping like a baby instead?"

"Absolutely not," he promised. "This time, expect me to kiss you from your ankles to your eyebrows, from sundown to sunup!"

They didn't have to wait, Maddie thought. Five days wasn't such a crucial length of time for healing, and she felt fine.

The truth was, the doctor's time frame gave them a badly needed chance to get to know each other again, in the quiet of their home. She and Sam had been married for a while; like musical notes written on a score, their song would play just as it always had, if they let it.

But she didn't want to fall into the rhythm they'd had before. Everything had changed in their lives, and as husband and wife, they had to change, too.

Or she'd never know if they were capable of withstanding the hard times in life. This time, she had to be sure.

"THE FIRST THING we have to do," Sam said, as soon as they got the babies into their cribs that night, "is talk."

"You're not much fun." Sam was right, but it was as if he'd read her mind, so Maddie resorted to teasing.

They seated themselves on the patio off the bedroom, the monitor nearby. She'd put her hair up with a green ribbon and changed into a long, slinky jade nightgown and bathrobe her mother had thoughtfully left in a wrapped box on her bed. "We love you, Maddie," the note read. "Here's a little something we thought Sam might like. Mom and Dad."

"We'll be all talked out in five days," Sam said, "and ready for action."

"Oh, I agree. I'm dressed for scintillating conversation." The sting was taken out of her words as she slid into his lap with a silky whisper of satin.

"Boy howdy," Sam said. "Your mom picked a doozy of a nightie." He ran a hand over the gown where it covered her thigh. "Almost as soft as your skin."

She laughed. "That won you a point."

They stared up at the stars for a moment, Maddie's head leaning against Sam's shoulder. The stars were pretty—tiny twinkles in a deep, dark sky—but her mind was on her husband. He had on a short-sleeved polo-style shirt, so that his bare forearms wrapped around her, anchoring her to him. His khaki shorts left much of his nicely built legs bare, and she could

feel the rougher texture of his skin through the soft-
ness of her gown. More than anything, she could feel
the steady hammer of his heart against her back, and
a pulse beating in his neck. He felt steady. Warm.
Secure.

''To be honest, Maddie, my goal isn't to score
points.''

She rolled her head so that she could see his face.
''What kind of talking do you want to do?''

He picked up her hand. ''I want to tell you five
things I wish I'd told you before.''

Her own pulse beat a little more quickly. ''I'm
listening.''

Pressing her forefinger against his lips, he said,
''Number one—I shouldn't have left you.''

''Oh, Sam.'' Her heart melted.

''Let me finish.''

She let the protest die on her lips as he kissed her
next finger.

''Two. I missed the hell out of you, Maddie. The
only reason I stayed gone was because I was hiding.''

''From what?'' she asked, her voice soft.

''From wanting you so badly and not being able
to give you what you wanted most.'' He brushed a
kiss against her temple. ''I was a little bit crazy from
feeling I should provide the things you needed. A
man ought to be able to give his woman a family.''

She lowered her eyes. ''We don't really know why
it didn't work for us, Sam. Maybe it just wasn't
meant to be at the time.''

He shook his head, then placed his lips against her

third finger. "Three—I love our babies. And I thank you for being braver than me."

"Braver? Or more headstrong?"

That brought a slightly wry grin to his face. "Both. It's a trait you come by honestly from Franny."

"I don't know that I was brave, Sam. Just…too scared not to try whatever medical help was available." She reached up to rest her hand against his cheek. "I should have told you, though. That was wrong of me."

"Which brings me to number four," he said, kissing and then nibbling her thumb. "I was very mad at you when I left. Then I was very angry with you when Joey told me what you'd done. I couldn't believe you would do something like that without telling me."

"I know." She felt tears sparkling in her eyes. "I'm afraid you're going to be a little more upset with me before the night is over. And you have every right to be."

He pulled away from her a little so that he could look directly at her. "You're not telling me you've kept some other secrets from me, are you?"

She winced. "Maybe one."

Sighing, he said, "Let me finish my last point for the night." He kissed her pinkie, and then her palm. "I just want you to know that no matter what you're about to tell me, I am not going to be angry. I am not getting upset. You are stuck with me for all eternity."

A smile lifted the corners of her mouth. "You're not hard to be stuck with."

Closing his eyes, he leaned his head back against the wrought-iron patio chair. "Boy, this talking stuff is exhausting."

She sat up. "Really? Supposedly talking is good for unburdening the soul."

"Maybe, but it opens up a whole new nest of problems that have to be talked about. We've got a lot of catching up to do."

"That's funny. I feel a lot better knowing what you've been keeping locked inside that hunky body of yours."

He opened one eye to stare at her. "Please, no flattery. I prefer my bad news without sugar, so shoot while I'm too worn-out to do much protesting."

Maddie took a deep breath, hating to have to tell him. "Thank you for sharing everything you just said. It means a lot to me, Sam."

He waited.

She shook his hand, and as he had, pressed a kiss to his forefinger. "Let's go back to point number four. About you being angry with me when Joey told you we'd had twins."

A brief nod was all the encouragement she received.

"Martin knew, too," she confessed in a broken whisper.

"Martin? Martin knew you were pregnant?" Sam sat straight up in the chair.

Her shoulders slumped. "Sam, I had to tell him. If anything had happened to me, well, you were still my husband legally, and—"

"Yes, damn it, I am! I was then and I am now." He stared at her. "My parents knew. My in-laws knew. And now you're telling me that my best friend and lawyer knew! I'm going to sue him. Heck, I'm going to kill him! I'm positive that's a breach of some kind of lawyer-client confidentiality.''

"Actually, I told him as a friend, Sam. But I made him promise he wouldn't tell you.'' She stared down at her hands. ''I wanted the chance to…''

Sam stared at his wife. Misery was etched on her pretty face. Her sable hair glistened in the light from the porch fixture and the candle she'd lit on the table. He could see tears shining in her eyes. But darn it, how could she be so sneaky? ''The chance to what?'' he demanded.

"I wanted you to have the chance to come back to me, Sam,'' she whispered. ''Without feeling like you had to.''

He felt as if he were carved from unyielding marble. Only his heart beat in his chest, a painful rhythm reminding him that he was flesh and blood. Capable of pain.

As she was.

"It's terrible when your husband leaves you,'' she said miserably. ''My heart broke when you walked out the door. I never knew I could hurt that bad.''

Their glances held in the shadowy light. He didn't know what to say. He was angry all over again, and the betrayal rubbed raw over the not entirely healed wounds of his heart.

She glanced away from him to stare down at her fingers, which she'd locked together. ''As hard as it was having to face that I couldn't have children, it was far worse losing my husband. I think I froze inside. It was too many losses to deal with all at once." She took a deep breath, exhaling heavily. "Sometimes I wondered why God was so unfair. Why I had to be crushed and torn, lose everything I'd dreamed of. To say that I fell into a depression is putting it mildly."

He'd known she was in pain. He'd been heartbroken, too. The misery their marriage had become had nearly made him crazy.

She looked at him, her face crumpled with doubt and regrets and painful memories.

"The only thing that gave me the strength to pull out of the black hole I'd fallen into was Dr. Maitland's phone call to tell me there was one more chance. One more chance to get everything back I'd lost."

Sam knew exactly the gut-wrenching fear she was talking about. But that didn't dilute the fresh pain he felt at her description. "I can't trust my wife, my parents or my lawyer," he said numbly. "You all ganged up on me." Pulling her chin so that she'd meet his eyes, he said, "Martin always says I'm his only honest client. But he wasn't honest with me."

"I'm not a client. I went to him as a friend I've known since high school. I went to him because you needed to know if something went wrong."

"But he's been lying to me." Sam shook his head. "I sent my deceitful lawyer over to France to run my company in my place. So I could be with my family. But he's disloyal. I can't trust him, and I can't trust you."

Tears slipped down Maddie's cheeks. "Don't say that, Sam. Martin loves you like a brother. He was terribly worried about how I was handling it. He never agreed that my way was the right way."

"Why did he fake it, then? Why did he suggest I have the babies tested for paternity?"

"He's your lawyer, Sam. He was advising you as he would any client, in case there had been a mistake."

"He should have told me, especially after Joey let the cat out of the bag. Martin could have mentioned that he'd known all along."

She wiped at her face, brushing at tears that kept coming. "This is my fault. Please don't blame him for something I did."

"And you want him to be the godfather to my children!" Sam said in a fresh burst of anger.

"Well, he and Vivi would make excellent godparents. All of our interests are tied together now, in the company, and after all the years we've been friends."

Sam shook his head. "I can't. I can forgive you because I understand why you did what you did. But I can't trust Martin now." He gritted his teeth, thinking. "I just realized I have six unscrupulous conspirators in France, supposedly guarding my best interests in a company I paid several million dollars for." He stared at her. "I'll have to fire Martin from Jardin. And switch my business to another lawyer."

"Sam!" Maddie sat up in his lap, her eyes pleading. "You can't be any less angry at me than him. He only did what I asked."

"I'm not," Sam said grimly. "I said I could forgive you, Maddie. I didn't say I have." Gently, he scooted her off his lap and stood. "I'm going to have to think about this. If you'll excuse me, I'll say goodnight.''

''Where are you going?'' she asked, rising too.

''Next door. I'll be over in the morning to relieve you from the babies.''

He left quickly, leaving through the gate in the fence between the two houses. She heard the door slam at his parent's place. Panic washed over her. It had been wrong of her, she knew. At the time, she'd thought she was doing the right thing. She'd wanted to keep her pregnancy to herself, unable to bear the thought of getting excited about it, only to have her hopes dashed. And then she'd waited too long, unable to breathe normally until she saw the two wonderful babies her body had actually been able to grow. Martin had pleaded with her to tell Sam.

Her fear had been too great. She was positive that if Sam wanted her, he would have returned to her. To their marriage.

Damn it, he wasn't going to walk out on her again, leaving her holding the pieces of her torn heart.

Chapter Twelve

Maddie stood for an indecisive moment. What was clear to her was that, this time, she was going after Sam. She would carefully explain to him in no uncertain terms that he could not walk out on her. "He has to come back," she muttered. "I'm not going to sit around and wait like I did before."

But she couldn't leave the babies. And she wasn't going to snatch them from a sound sleep to drag them next door. Her romantic nightgown and robe weren't appropriate attire for dragging a furious husband back—nor for letting off her own steam. If the neighbors saw her standing on his front porch in her nightgown, banging on the door, they would certainly wonder about her sanity.

She pulled off her robe, jerked off her gown and reached for a pair of jeans. The sliding glass door opened abruptly.

"Aiiee!" she gasped, whirling around, the jeans pressed to her chest.

"Where are you going?" Sam demanded.

He came back! her heart sang. "For a walk," she hedged.

"Oh."

He took that in for a second before crossing his arms over his chest. His gaze scanned the blue jeans and the skin they didn't cover. A blush sizzled over her nearly nude body. "If you could give me a moment," she said, her tone cool.

"Certainly."

He turned away, but it was obvious he could see her reflection in the sliding door, since the lamps were on inside the bedroom, highlighting it against the darkness outside.

She wouldn't give him the satisfaction. Marching into the bathroom, she slid into her jeans and snatched a top from the master closet. Taking a deep breath to compose herself, she walked back into the bedroom. "Was there something you came back for?"

"I'm sorry," he said simply.

Her anger at his retreat began to fade with those words.

"I shouldn't have walked out. I am upset. I *will* kick Martin's butt over this, eventually. But I was the one who suggested that you and I needed to talk, and I shouldn't have lost my temper."

"I knew you'd be mad," she admitted. "I'm sorry, Sam."

"No. The truth is, I'm not upset with you for confiding in Martin, because that's what I would have wanted you to do for the sake of the children we were expecting. I'm not angry at Martin for keeping your confidence, because I know he wanted us to get back together as much as our parents did." Sam took a deep breath. "To be honest, I'm irate with myself, because you couldn't tell me what you told Martin. And that's no one's fault but mine.''

"Ours,'' she reminded him.

An instant passed before he nodded. "Okay. Ours.''

They looked at each other for a long moment, and Maddie could feel her heart squeezing with joy that he'd come back, and that they'd made it over a very painful hurdle.

"Even more humiliatingly honest, I had a gut re-action of jealousy,'' he admitted.

Her eyebrows shot up. "Of Martin?'' she asked incredulously. "I've known him since he was a skinny high school geek wearing horn-rims.''

Sam snorted. "Don't remind me.''

"There's nothing to be jealous of, Sam.''

He looked shamefaced. "I know. As I said, it was momentary, blind and stupid. Martin adores you, but as even he has said, it's in a little-sister fashion. I guess that's hard for me to relate to, since there's nothing about you I find little-sisterly.''

"Trust me, if Martin and I were stranded together on an island for five years, all we would do is play chess with seashells and checkers with coconuts. That's it.''

He smiled ruefully. "I knew that. I realized as soon as my front door slammed that the feeling I had was ego-driven. And selfish.''

"So?'' She slanted an eyebrow at him.

"I came back.''

With a smile, she went into his arms. "Good thing, too, because the destination of my walk was to drag you out of your cave. The neighbors would have gotten quite a show.''

He looked down into her eyes. ''I wouldn't have had to be dragged. Well, I might have put up a little resistance just so I could enjoy the knowledge of you wanting me bad enough to…you know. Come after me. Fight for me.''

She glimpsed the pain of their separation in his eyes. ''Did you want me to come after you when you were in France?''

Breathing in deeply through his nose, he said, ''Yeah. After a while, I wanted to be rescued from my pride.''

Maddie nodded. She knew how that felt. Laying her head on his chest, she held him closely for a long time.

Upstairs, a baby's cry erupted.

She smiled at the shattering sound. ''Night duty, after all.''

Sam followed her up the stairs. ''We'll have to ask them to sleep without a wake-up call Saturday night. I want you to myself.''

Maddie laughed. ''I heard a rumor that children never do what their parents want them to do. It's something parents fight against until the kids turn about…oh, thirty.''

''Don't tell me any more,'' Sam said with a groan. ''I just know my boys will be sympathetic to the night their father has been impatiently waiting for.'' He caught her hand before she picked up an infant. ''I'd like to do this again tomorrow night.''

''We're doing it for a week.''

''I mean talk. I think we should make a date to

talk every night until the big night. As if we were simply dating again." He kissed her hand. "I want our marriage to work."

Her heart thundered in a new, hopeful beat. "You were a pretty decent date once upon a time."

"I was a great date! You liked going out with me."

It was true. Sam had been the only man she had enjoyed dating. She gave him a coy smile. "It was better than washing my hair."

He grinned at her. "Tomorrow night, I'm going to make you take that back and admit that you couldn't wait for me to call."

She pulled her hand away and scooped up Henry, who had quieted momentarily when they'd walked into the room. Sam picked up Hayden, who seemed content to suck his fist for the moment. Sam and Maddie sat next to each other in the bentwood rockers.

"It wasn't your phone call I couldn't wait for," Maddie said softly. "It was your lovemaking that kept me on pins and needles for our next date."

"Shh!" Sam said. "Not in front of my sons!" He held Hayden close, kissing his forehead. "What would you think about your mother and father enjoying the fruits of marriage before we visited the altar?" he asked the baby. "Especially when we're going to tell you to wait. And wait. And wait. But if either of you boys finds a woman like your mother," Sam said to his sons, "I'll completely understand!"

SAM THOUGHT ABOUT what Maddie had said as he made certain each baby was covered with a light blanket. Making love with Maddie had been excellent. They were totally in tune with each other's desires and needs, like perfect reflections.

It was beyond him, and it always would be, how two people who enjoyed the passion that they'd known were unable to produce children the old-fashioned way. When he made love to Maddie, he'd felt like every part of his body exploded in a breath-stealing, soul-stopping current of endless pleasure.

"It doesn't matter," he whispered to his sons. "Your old dad just needed a little help getting you here. But every time I made love to your mother, I was making you. Every single time."

He was telling them the truth.

There was one overwhelming thing he had to tell Maddie before the big night. It was very important, and it had to do with future babies.

"I DON'T THINK I'm going to get my prepregnancy figure back like this," Maddie groaned, eyeing the bedside clock, which read an unfortunate 6:00 a.m. "I'm too exhausted to exercise!"

Both of them lay flat on their backs, staring at the ceiling after falling across the bed. The babies had awakened every hour on the hour, restless in their cribs. One would wake and cry, and that would get his twin started.

Maddie didn't think she could make love right now if her life depended on it. Physically, she felt like she couldn't walk.

"Your prepregnancy figure will come back in time," Sam said, a dead weight beside her. "It's my forty-two-year-old frame that would retaliate if I asked it to jog today.''

She rolled her head to look at her husband. ''You're in pretty good shape for a middle-aged guy. I'd still pick you up at a bar.''

He laughed at the stock routine they'd repeated many times in the past. ''Maddie, you'd have to. I'm your husband. Anyone else would merely be a cheap imitation.''

She covered his hand with hers. ''But did you ever think we might find other loves?''

This was a deviation from the routine. He raised an eyebrow at her, and she raised hers back in challenge.

''No,'' he said definitely. ''Even though our marriage fell apart, I never stopped loving you. I couldn't have remotely allowed my brain to think about you with another man. In fact, the thought of it is paining my gut right now. Can we change the subject?''

''I guess so. If you're uncomfortable.'' She winked at him.

He wrinkled his mouth before sighing heavily. ''Maddie, one of the reasons I liked France was because I wouldn't have to deal with some schmuck realizing what a great woman you are.''

She stared at him. ''You went to France for the wine.''

''Yes. And I stayed because I knew I couldn't handle anyone else…being with you.'' Clasping her fingers between his, he said, ''It would have happened eventually. What could I do? Drop in every once in a while and pretend like we were friends? Live down the block and try to tell myself I didn't want to hold you at night?'' He snorted. ''I'm only so much man.''

''You be lotsa man, ba-bay,'' she teased.

''Not enough, it seemed at the time.''

She rolled over and placed her head on Sam's chest. ''We got what we wanted, Sam. Those little babies upstairs that kept us up all night, remember?'' She smiled. ''Adorable, and a little more than we bargained for.''

''With you, that has always been the case. I've always gotten just a *little* bit more than I bargained for.''

She slapped at him before getting up and pulling him down to the floor. ''It's time to work out. Nearly six weeks after birth, and I'm still thirty pounds overweight.''

''I can handle the extra load. Forget about it. Anyway, if you're packing that much extra, I don't know where it's hiding.'' He ogled her deliberately. ''Except of course, your breasts. Now, I can definitely see that my sons are being fed well—''

''Sit like this.'' She spread her legs and reached for his hands. ''Put your feet against mine.''

''This is not the way I want my feet against yours,'' he grumbled, but he complied anyway, clasping her hands and forming a diamond shape with their legs.

''Now rock,'' she instructed.

''Band on the run,'' he sang, bobbing his head to imaginary music. ''Band on the run!''

''Not Beatles. Rock *yourself.*''

''Can I rock you instead? You like that, you know.''

She narrowed her gaze on him. "Sam, pay attention. We rock that way Saturday night. But for the moment, rock back and forth on your admirable buns, and pull me forward gently when you do."

He sighed. "As much as it sounds like sex, it's not. You're determined to give me rug burn the only way I don't want to get it." But he pulled, tugging her forward, and then she seesawed back, pulling him.

Slowly, they tested the feel of the motion, enjoying the sense of working together. After he'd pulled her forward about ten times, he said, "I change my mind. This is fun."

"You're looking down my nightgown," she said, huffing. "But if it keeps you working, help yourself."

"You're only saying that because you know I got an erection the instant you leaned over."

She started giggling, and he kept her pulled forward so he could stare down the gaping material. "I've got an even better idea for our physical fitness. Let's do this nude," he suggested.

"I give up," she said, releasing his hands. "You have no focus."

"I have *intense* focus. What do you want me to say after nine months, Maddie? Gee, what lovely breasts you have, and you look like a fabulous Reubens painting I saw in the Louvre, but you don't turn me on?"

She looked at him suspiciously. "You don't think I'm fat?"

He pulled hard, a slow tug that brought her close enough to him that he could grab her waist and jerk her forward onto him. "Nah, I can still manhandle you."

Snorting, she said, "Shall you be punished for that remark now or later?"

A shrill baby cry suddenly filtered through the speaker. They both got to their knees and looked at the TV monitor. Two little heads were moving against the sheets, tiny fingers beginning to flex in agitation.

"I guess it'll have to be later," Sam said.

"Wonder why these little dickens can't sleep?" Maddie asked as Sam helped her to her feet.

"They miss the warm, comforting bosoms of grandmothers. You'll miss them, too, if this keeps up."

She glanced over her shoulder at him as they hurried up the stairs. "Do you wish our moms were here?"

"Nope. But I've got the bosom I love nearby." He tweaked her bottom playfully, making her hurry faster up the stairs to get away from him. "See, and I've even shown you a better way to become fit more quickly. Stair leaping."

Maddie shook her head at him as she picked up Hayden, who was close to working himself into a full lather. "I think some chauvinism crept into you while you were in France. Obviously you were away much too long," she told him, her eyes snapping with heightened passion at his teasing.

"I know," he said simply. "It's clear as anything that you missed me."

"What makes you say that, especially as I was just running away from you?"

"Sometimes running away is just wanting to be caught."

They looked at each other. "Maybe one day I'll let you catch me," she said softly.

"I'll make it worth your while," he promised.

THAT AFTERNOON they had a photo shoot scheduled with the founder of Maitland Maternity. Henry and Hayden were a miracle Maitland wanted to showcase. But it was clear to Sam that his wife was nervous and edgy. Neither of them had slept much last night, and the infants were fussy.

He thought about suggesting to Maddie that they reschedule the session. She needed rest more than she needed to be carting irritable babies around. But this was important to her because of what Maitland had given her, and so it was important to him.

Yawning, he packed diapers and wipes into a baby bag. "I must be getting old," he said to his sons, who were listening to the sound of his voice from their places on the king-size bed. "Funny, I really didn't feel old until I started getting up every hour or so with you guys."

Henry and Hayden lay between pillows on their backs, waving their tiny arms every once in a while. They were dressed like little princes in matching blue sailor onesies, with white booties on their feet. Sam smiled. "Maybe an outing will wear you little guys out so you can rest better," he said. Sitting on the edge of the bed, he rubbed the back of his neck and then massaged across his chest. "I know you're wearing me out," he told them.

Henry let out an indignant wail.

"Oh, no, it's all right. I didn't mean to begrudge you your right to keep me hopping," he told him, lying down between his sons. "It's hard to believe that two six-pound fellas with toes no bigger than…" He inspected his sons' tiny booties. "Well, let's just say I've seen baby peas that are bigger than your toes. How such minute little men can throw my entire world into utter chaos is something I can't figure out."

They turned toward his low, soothing murmuring so he rolled them onto their stomachs. First he watched Henry, and then he turned his head to look at Hayden. Being on their stomachs settled them, and after a moment, they began sucking their fists. Sam glanced back and forth between them a second longer, feeling his eyelids grow heavier and heavier. He could hear Maddie splashing in the bathroom, or maybe it was that spitting statue she liked so much.

Whatever it was, the sound was mesmerizing. He let his tired eyes close, just for a moment. *I won't really fall asleep, I have to get dressed so I can play the proud papa—which won't be terribly difficult.*

If he snoozed for just a second, the indigestion he'd been feeling for the past couple of hours would subside. And then he'd make Maddie sleep tonight while he slept upstairs with the boys. They'd all have frozen dinners for supper. He'd have a Hungry Man because the indigestion would be gone by then, and his sons could have a baggie of breast milk, nicely warmed to a temperature comparable to Mom's.

The thought brought a smile to his face as he drifted off.

Chapter Thirteen

Maddie came out of the bathroom and smiled at her boys nestled beside their father. Her insides shivered. Two months ago, she would never have dreamed that Sam would return to her, and be such a loving father and husband.

Nine months ago, she wouldn't have dared to dream that she'd be pregnant. "I'm so blessed," she whispered, tracing gentle fingers through Sam's dark hair. It lay at his nape as he snored rhythmically, the side of his face pressed into the white lace comforter. Henry and Hayden were sleeping deeply, their tiny bodies adorable in their sailor outfits.

It was probably unfortunate that they'd fallen into a restful sleep just when they needed to leave the house. She hated to wake them, or Sam, for that matter. He hadn't seemed as energetic this morning as he had in the past few weeks. Of course, they were both running on lack of sleep. But Sam was used to jet lag and international time differences. It surprised her that he seemed so run-down. Usually she was the one who had energy leaking out of her like an old battery.

"Sam, wake up," she murmured softly. "We need to get to the hospital for the photo shoot."

He opened one eye and groaned.

"I'm sorry." She stroked her fingers along the side of his face, somehow still amazed that he was here with her and that she could touch him to her heart's content. "Why don't I go by myself so you can catch up on some sleep?"

"No. I'm fine." His eye closed.

When he didn't move, Maddie frowned. Sam had never been as lethargic as this. He definitely needed rest. Quietly, she gathered the babies' things and carried them out to the car. Then she lifted Henry and took him to his carrier, next securing Hayden. Putting her purse over her shoulder, she lifted the babies out onto the porch stoop and closed the door ever so stealthily.

She was just transferring the last baby carrier into the car when Sam came hopping out the front door, fastening his khaki trousers as he hurried to juggle shoes, socks and his keys to lock the door. "Maddie! Wait!"

"I can do this by myself. I'd rather you stay here and get some rest, Sam."

"No way. You shouldn't be carrying heavy things, and I can't miss my boys' first modeling session."

Maddie shook her head at him wryly. "Henry and Hayden can hardly be classified as tonnage. And it's just Megan Maitland we're seeing, not a Hollywood talent scout."

"All the more reason I need to be with you, then." He jumped into the passenger seat and slammed the door. "The picture of a happy family isn't complete without Dad."

"They're not interested in our pictures, Sam, just the babies'." But Maddie shook her head again, smiling. She finished making certain the car seats were appropriately situated. The carriers faced backward, and the seat belts were snugly in place. Satisfied, she opened the drivers' door and slid behind the wheel.

"Can you drive?" Sam asked.

"Yes." She gave him a curious look.

"But did Dr. Abby okay it?"

"Yes, Sam." She switched on the ignition.

"Do you mind driving? I need to finish dressing, but if you give me five seconds, I'll have my shoes on—"

"Sam. You're overdoing the protective routine. Please." She pulled away from the curb, driving slowly. "I do wish you'd stay and rest."

"If anybody needs sleep, it's you. You're the open-all-night diner." He took a deep breath, running both hands through his hair in an attempt to tame it, but the brown strands pretty much defied the attempt.

"You look fine. It's the boys who are the stars."

"Yes, but I want to talk to these Maitland people."

She glanced at him. "What about?"

He shrugged. "It's time for me to express my thanks for what they gave me."

She blinked and was about to reply when he continued, "And I'm going to tell them that my wife and I will probably be interested in utilizing their services again in the near future.''

Her lips parted. Unnerved, she pulled over to the curb in front of a neighbor's house. She turned to stare at her husband. "You told me you weren't going to—"

He held up a palm. "I know what I said." Scrubbing at the back of his neck for a second, he grimaced. "Those little guys back there, and you, mean the world to me. I can't imagine a time when I didn't have you, all of you." Shaking his head, he said, "Well, I don't want to remember when it was just me, living by myself, putting everything I had into a business that isn't going to matter in the long run as much as this family does.''

"Oh, Sam.'' Maddie glanced away from his gaze for just a moment, her heart too full to speak.

He covered her shoulder with his palm, before sliding it up to cup her neck. "All I know is that despite sleep deprivation, despite the fact we stay in that house most of the time and somehow manage to run what I know must be a marathon of miles chasing diapers and bottles and wipes and pacifiers, I'm happy. I'm exhausted, but I wouldn't trade it for the world.''

She smiled at him. "They *have* rearranged our world.''

"That they have." He looked at her for a long moment. "And I guess all I'm trying to say is that if you decide you need another Maitland miracle, I'm not going to let my pride stand in the way. If nature didn't give me everything I needed to hit the target properly, then I don't mind a little assistance with my aim.''

She reached over to hug him, and they held each other for a long time. Maddie closed her eyes and told herself there was more than one miracle Maitland had performed.

SAM FOUND HIMSELF respectfully impressed as he met the Maitland clan. Megan Maitland, the Maitland Maternity founder, was there, as well as Mitchell. Dr. Abby was on hand for the photo shoot. All of these people cared about his wife and his children.

Somehow, that took the last sting out of his pride. They were genuinely caring people who didn't seem to think less of him for being away when his children were born.

Rubbing a palm over his chest surreptitiously, Sam enjoyed watching his babies being adored by a group of nurses. Maddie was complimented for how well she looked. He liked hearing that. It made him feel as if they thought he was taking good care of her, which he'd certainly tried to do. His stubborn little wife was pretty certain she could do everything on her own, but he planned to remind her often that it took two of them to tango, and it would take two of them to raise their family. Nothing had been said as yet of them staying together for good. He hadn't wanted to push the issue. But it was almost time for him to convince Maddie that she'd be a lot happier with him than without him.

Maybe he should ask her to marry him again. Technically, they were still married, but somehow, it didn't seem the same to him, and he knew it didn't seem the same to her. They had been separated too long. Watching his wife as she walked across the room, he admired the way the red pantsuit fit her. Her gleaming, mahogany chin-length hair swinging, she moved with confidence, gesturing as she talked.

His jaw dropped. She wasn't wearing her wedding band! The strange pain that had been in his chest suddenly intensified. Why had he not noticed that before? He still wore *his*.

He'd been thinking all week about his surprise for her—the moment he was going to tell her that he'd been wrong, that they most definitely should have more children. When he had done so, she hadn't said anything. She'd only hugged him.

He sat heavily in one of the chairs situated around the big room. The breath seemed to roll out of him as if pressed. Then he couldn't draw any back into his body. Sweat broke out on his forehead. His hands suddenly felt clammy, cool.

Maddie turned around and smiled at him, a bright sexy smile meant only for him, and the pain lifted so that he could breathe. He leaned back in the chair, telling himself he was simply tired.

"Fine boys you've got there," Mitchell Maitland said, taking the seat next to Sam.

"I've got you to thank for them," Sam said. "Maddie and I may one day go this route again."

Mitchell frowned. "What route, Sam?"

"You know." Sam shifted uncomfortably, not certain of his words. "Whatever it was you did that made us able to conceive."

The doctor looked at him steadily for a few seconds. "Did Maddie tell you she wanted to have another procedure?"

Now Sam frowned. "We discussed it."

Mitchell wrinkled up his eyes, clearly choosing his words carefully. "I'll have to talk to her about this, then. It hadn't occurred to me that Maddie would want more children, since she had twins."

"I think she wants to get on the fast track because she's getting closer to forty. She'd like one more baby."

"I see."

Sam swallowed, his throat pinching. "For some reason, you don't sound enthusiastic about her desire for another procedure."

Mitchell slowly shook his head. "I need to talk to her about it, Sam. But as her husband, you might be the best one to encourage her to be happy with the two wonderful babies she has."

The pain crept into his chest again, maddening in its refusal to subside completely. Sam ignored it. "What are you saying, Dr. Maitland? Bottom line?"

Mitchell sighed. "I couldn't advise you to risk it again. It wouldn't be fair to the children she has."

"Are you saying Maddie put herself in a high-risk situation before?" The agony inside his rib cage intensified until it felt like a hot stone he couldn't dislodge.

"It was risky," Mitchell said, "but Maddie was determined. At her age, it wasn't something I ringingly endorsed. I knew how much it meant to her. I also knew that her inability to conceive had virtually ruined your marriage," he said, lowering his voice confidentially. "The truth was, at that time, Maddie had a lot more to gain than to lose. Now that simply isn't the case.''

No, it wasn't. Not for Sam, either. He was a happy man, a deeply satisfied man.

Across the room, Maddie laughed, the sound rich and yet heartbreakingly feminine. He would give anything he could to make her happy.

She wasn't wearing her wedding band. Their marriage had deteriorated over their inability to become pregnant. Now a renowned physician was telling him that the procedure that had probably saved his marriage and given him back his wife wasn't available to them anymore.

The painful thought hit him that she'd been right; their reborn relationship hadn't really been tested, hadn't been welded into one undividable bond.

The air around him grew hot. Maddie glanced his way, her large green eyes laughing, her face beautiful with its natural complexion and the girlish appeal Martin described as little sisterish, but which had always been erotically womanly to Sam—and the next thing he knew, his chest erupted in fiery anguish.

''REST. Plenty of it. And relaxation,'' Maddie told Sam as he lay in a hospital bed. ''Doctor's orders.''

He groaned, having been through a series of tests ranging from a simple electrocardiogram to more complicated ones he couldn't pronounce. All to tell him he needed rest. ''You need sleep more than I do,'' he rasped.

She smiled. ''You're suffering angina brought on by...the babies and me.''

"Uh-uh." He shook his head against the pillow. "Without you three, I'm nothing."

"With us, you're going to have a heart attack." She leaned over to kiss his forehead.

He caught her hand, pulling her into the bed beside him so that he could hold her. "Now, I'm healed."

She laughed. "Sam, you're supposed to be taking it easy!"

"I can't. Where are my sons?"

"With nurses who fawn upon their every baby command." Frowning up at him, she said, "Sam, your mother left a message at the house."

"Oh, no."

Maddie didn't meet his gaze immediately. "Yes. And so I returned her call."

"You didn't tell her, did you? She'll be over here on the next plane to take care of me." He shook his head, perplexed. "She does have some maternal prescience, just as we thought. Only hers is so strong that she even picks up vibes across an ocean." He mused for a moment. "There is the possibility that my mom's prescience is fusing with yours, combining for a max-powerful ESP force not seen before on planet earth. We'll never be out of their reach!"

He was going to have a colossal fit when she told him what Sara had called about. "Well..."

He raised up on an elbow to stare at her. "Look. I have stress-related angina. I don't need our parents back here stirring things up. We haven't had enough time alone."

Maddie pushed him back onto the pillow. "Breathe deeply, Sam. Relax. I'm going to spring you out of here in just a few moments."

"You're not answering my question."

Sighing, she eased herself to a sitting position and stared down at him. "I didn't know what to say to her, Sam. I knew if I didn't call her back immediately, she and my mom would start wondering why we weren't at home with the babies. The message was left hours ago. They know the babies would be at home for naps. I had to call."

"And so? What did you tell them?"

"Nothing," she said softly.

"You're pulling my leg." His deep blue eyes held a worried expression.

"I didn't know what you'd want me to say. I told them everything was fine."

He covered her hand with his. "Most of it is fine."

She raised a brow. "What isn't fine?"

"You and me."

When she didn't say anything, he sighed. "We need more time."

"We're not going to get more time if you die of a heart attack on me."

"It was angina brought on by worry and exhaustion. I'm forty-two, not a *GQ* cover model in my studly twenties. It's an unwieldy fact I'd rather not face, but…you should be home with the babies. You shouldn't be here."

"Shh." She put her head down on his chest and listened to the steady sound of his heart. "It sounds all right in there."

"It's the heart of a chicken, obviously."

"It's the heart of a man who would do anything for his family. I'd call that more lion than chicken." She raised her head to look at him once more. "But even lions get tired, Sam. The truth is, I should call your mother back and—''

''No!'' He held up his palms. ''I realize I'm being a little selfish, because you could use better assistance than mine, but—''

''No, I actually couldn't.''

They looked at each other for a long time.

''You scared me to death,'' she finally told him. ''I thought you were going to leave me here with two young sons who would never know their father.''

He snorted. ''Not a chance. I'm an almost perfect physical specimen.''

''Who needs to exercise more, rest more and stop worrying so much.''

''See?'' he said, his hand closing over hers. ''Sex is the best exercise in the world. It will help me rest. And then I'll stop worrying. I think you'd better move me back in with you permanently.''

She smiled, dropping a kiss on his forehead. ''Sam, I have a couple of things I have to tell you, but now is not the time.''

A frown drew lines in his forehead. ''I have something to tell you, too. Mine's not good,'' he warned. ''What's yours?''

''Not good, either,'' she admitted. ''But I'm afraid if I tell you, you'll…not take it well.''

''Sam the baby. Baby Sam. He's going to have a little chest pain if he hears bad news. Nothing could be that bad.'' *Especially compared to what I have to tell you, which is going to do more than stir up a little angina.*

Dr. Maitland's advice against another surgically assisted pregnancy.

It was going to break her heart.

Chapter Fourteen

"I guess you could say our parents have taken a shine to running your winery," Maddie said as rapidly as possible. If she summoned her flagging courage and forced herself to tell him quickly, maybe the whole matter would blow over that much sooner.

Sam rolled his eyes. "If it keeps them out of our hair, huzzah. How much damage can they do in a week?"

Maddie swallowed. "Your mother wanted to know if we needed her—"

"The answer is unequivocally no. I hope you told her as gently as possible."

"I did. I said they should stay in France as long as they liked."

He raised an eyebrow. "Stay in France? The plane tickets were for one week."

"And they wanted to know if you minded them cashing in the return section of the tickets. They're not ready to come home yet. They'll pay to get themselves home."

"Well." Sam pushed himself up in the bed before swinging his legs over so he could put on his shoes.

"I'm surprised. Bless Vivi and Martin for being such good hosts."

Maddie wrinkled up her mouth and scrunched her nose, contemplating Sam's good humor. The last thing she wanted to do was upset him, but he was going to find out sooner or later. "Sam, apparently our parents are causing a bit of a sensation in the land of supreme vintage."

"If you're trying to tell me in a roundabout way that my folks and Joey have passed out under picnic tables somewhere along the Seine due to their consumption of excellent wine, it's fine, Maddie. I'm not going to have a massive infarction over my folks enjoying themselves."

"They're going to be on the cover of *Wine* magazine," Maddie said miserably.

Sam stared at her. "The cover?"

"Apparently they're quite a hit. The article was titled something like 'Brash and Wealthy Texas Family Pulls a Corporate Coup and Finds Themselves Romanced by France's Most Famous Winery.'"

A tiny smile tugged at his face. "You're not serious."

"Well, perhaps I don't have the title quite right," Maddie admitted. "But that was the gist."

Sam began to laugh.

"What's so funny?" she asked suspiciously.

"That. It's funny. I don't know why. I can see our moms on the cover with little cap pistols and our dads waving cowboy hats."

"I see nothing funny about being a laughing-stock," Maddie said stiffly. "They're ruining the company you wanted so badly."

"It's good PR. I probably couldn't have bought that kind of publicity."

Maddie shook her head, amazed by Sam's attitude. "I feel embarrassed."

He shrugged. "You shouldn't. But if it makes you feel better, I'll talk to Vivi and Martin and make sure our folks aren't causing more trouble than good."

"I would appreciate that." She saw nothing good about the matter, but the possibility of upsetting Sam had given her the most concern. "I just don't understand why my parents can't go on a simple vacation without stirring things up. Why can't they be normal parents? Is it too much to ask that they sit demurely on an airplane somewhere and show off photos of their grandkids? They could go to France and behave like normal tourists, snapping pictures of the Eiffel Tower and trying French phrases on the locals. But no. Not my parents."

"I've said this before and I'll say it again, my parents are in it up to their ears. I think they make a fun foursome."

"Joey is supposed to keep them out of trouble," Maddie said sternly. "According to your mother, the interviewer *loved* my brother's beefy bod. He posed with a wine bottle, wearing only a towel, for the inside section of the magazine. Like a centerfold, darn it." She ground her teeth. "But even worse, apparently, Joey and the interviewer are now engaged in the hottest romance France has seen in quite a while."

"Nah. France has seen so many hot ones the people are used to fanning the flames." Sam's chuckle turned into a full-blown laugh. He laughed so hard his face turned blush-red along the cheekbones and so did his neck, upsetting Maddie all over again.

"Mother even mentioned that they might split the purchase of a small château with your folks, Sam. They're going way over the line."

"Actually, that would be much nicer than staying in a hotel."

"Sam! It's awfully flighty of them, don't you think?"

"No. We heard them say they wanted to do fun things in their retirement. Splitting the cost of a château would give them someplace nice to visit when they liked. Frankly, it's a great idea, honey. We could have a place to stay when we go over there on business. My flat is fine for one, but with the babies, we'd be better off with more room."

She frowned. "It just seems like they're jumping in with both feet."

"Yeah, well, maybe you're just envious. We haven't done any jumping with both feet in some time. To be honest, we should probably offer to go in on whatever house they choose. That way the cost would be split in thirds. Time-sharing is cost-effective, anyway." He shrugged. "Maybe it's time we think about a vacation ourselves. The babies are nearly six weeks old. They'll start to settle into a rhythm soon and we can take them with us. What do you say?"

"Let's just get you home for now," she stated, suddenly all-business. "Any more news flashes from our parents and you're going to spend the extra time they're gone in the hospital."

His grin slipped from his face and he stared at her for a long moment.

"Are you all right?" she demanded.

Waving her concern away, he said, "I'm fine. Just take me home. We need to talk."

Her heart started beating uncomfortably in her chest. He looked so serious Maddie became worried again. As it was, she felt like a year had been taken off her life—Sam had scared her with his sudden chest pains.

The nurses had fed the babies some formula when they'd gotten hungry, which had filled their stomachs so that they slept like lambs. Maddie resolved to cease breast-feeding so the babies wouldn't get up every two hours, which would help with the sleep deprivation she and Sam were suffering. And she promised herself to get a mother's helper if they needed one. She'd leaped at the opportunity to keep their parents in France where they were out of their hair, though not totally out of trouble.

What could make Sam look so sad?

Maybe he'd gotten bad news on one of the medical tests. Her blood ice-cold, Maddie shook her head. "You have to do nothing but rest when we get home."

"After we talk we'll both try to get some zee's. But this is important, Maddie."

"AMAZING," Maddie said. "Maybe they're worn out from all the extra attention they received. And from being up all last night."

The babies lay in their cribs, their bodies motionless for once as they slumbered. They hadn't awakened in the car, nor during the transfer from car seat to crib. "I'd like to see you tucked into bed like them," she added to Sam.

"Don't baby me, Maddie. I know you're concerned, but there's more to think about than some minor exhaustion and stress."

She tugged his hand so that he'd follow her down the stairs. Steering him into the bedroom, she edged him toward the bed. Without much prodding, he stretched out there, but he pulled her with him, almost on top of him.

"Now this would make me feel better," he said, nuzzling her.

"Stop!" she said, laughing as she tried to push him away. "You need to sleep, Sam."

He nipped at her shoulder and rubbed a swift hand over her blouse. "These clothes must come off. And be aware that I know you're trying to sidetrack me."

"I'm trying to sidetrack you!" she cried with a yelp as he helped her out of her trousers more swiftly than she was expecting. "I think you're trying to get out of following doctor's orders."

"He said to exercise and to try to decompress." Sam swiftly removed her blouse so that she was wearing only a bra and panties. "There's only one way I know of to achieve both those goals at once."

"Is that so?" She tugged off his shoes and then his khakis before helping herself to his shirt. He had a wonderful chest. How could that magnificent body be covering up a heart in pain? "Sam, you should have told me you weren't feeling well today. I knew you were worn-out, but you never mentioned chest pain."

"And you never mentioned the two little things sleeping upstairs, little woman, a fact I grappled with and got over." He kissed her on the nose. "I didn't keep it from you purposefully. To tell you the truth, I thought it was indigestion made a bit worse by the fact that I'm somewhat crazed from lack of sleep. I want to forget about it, Maddie. Let's get down to decompressing."

She shook her head. "I want you to go to sleep."

"I want to have some fun. I want to laugh for a change, Maddie. With you. I want to see you smile. I want us to jump into the joy of life with both feet. I think our parents are on to something."

He looked so sad and serious Maddie's heart nearly broke. "Okay," she said, taking hold of his hand. "Come on." She pulled him up so that they were standing on the king-size bed.

"What are we doing?"

"Decompressing. Go!" She began jumping up and down maniacally.

He watched her for a moment as the bed shifted erratically under her feet.

"Come on!" she exclaimed.

When she landed a flat-bottomed seat drop and flew back to stand on her feet, Sam decided she was having too much fun. "Okay. Watch the pro," he bragged, jumping so high he nearly bounced her off the bed.

She shrieked with laughter as the challenge began in earnest. They took turns trying to see who could out-bounce the other, chasing each other around the bed like boxing partners.

"This is what the doctor had in mind," Maddie

gasped breathlessly, "when he told you to decompress. Jumping on the bed is forbidden by parents, it's good exercise and it takes you back to stress-free childhood days."

Still jumping, Sam said, "I'm pretty sure it would be even more fun if you were completely naked. I still say we should always exercise without constricting garments."

"Never!" Maddie jumped far away from him, clear to the opposite side of the bed so that she could hop onto the carpet. "Jumping on the bed is immature enough. We don't have to make a nudist sport of it."

He made a ferocious leap, clearing the bed and landing beside her so that she squealed. "Sam! You're going to have a heart attack if you're not careful!"

"My arteries are clear. My heart pumps just fine." He grabbed her, picking her up in his arms like Tarzan carrying Jane from the jungle. "I just need to get inside my wife and I'll be cured. The doctor said sex was the best exercise I could indulge in, and it would help me sleep. Doctor's orders."

"It wasn't! The doctor said no such thing." But she looked at him saucily, her heart beating hot and fast, and not just from the sudden workout. "I thought you had something you wanted to talk about."

His gaze shifted instantly away from her, the fun in the moment evaporating like steam.

"What's bothering you, Sam? You have to tell me. We have to learn to lean on each other."

He shook his head after a moment. "You know

what? I might be a little sleepy. Let's get some shut-eye while the tots are getting theirs.''

They got in bed, and Sam pressed up against her back.

A few seconds later, he snored. Maddie was thrilled he was going to get some rest, but a nagging thought ground away at her. Sam had never, ever gone to sleep pressed up against her back when she wore only a bra and panties. They'd had a great sex life before they'd tried to start having children. It was the routine and the disappointments that made making love a chore had helped to shatter their marriage.

She bit her lip. Something was bothering Sam deeply. It was either his health or something more sinister. He'd said they needed to talk.

The bed-jumping had been the most exuberant and spontaneous fun they'd had recently, a badly needed moment of shared happiness.

The instant she'd reminded him that he had something to tell her, he'd lost his smile. He'd closed off from her almost totally.

It bothered her terribly, and hurt her, too, that Sam had a problem he didn't feel he could share with her. Which was what she'd been afraid of all along—that they were only making their relationship work because of the children, and their marriage couldn't survive another major roadblock.

She didn't think she could stand the heartbreak. When Sam had gone so suddenly pale as he'd sat next to Dr. Maitland, she'd known something was wrong, even before Mitchell had called for a nurse to help Sam to an examining room.

Maddie's own heart had seemed to nearly explode

with fear. When the doctor called for a cardiologist, Maddie had struggled not to faint. In that split second, it had hit her with crystal clarity how much Sam mattered to her. Everything that had happened in the past fled her mind, and none of it mattered: not the disastrous feelings of inadequacy she'd suffered, not the long months of separation. Sam had come back to her, and she had known hope again. Her soul had been in agony that he might be suffering a heart attack that might take him away from her.

Now he was pushing her away emotionally if not physically—and she felt lost beyond words.

They were under one roof together—and yet somehow still alone.

Chapter Fifteen

"You're doing fine," Dr. Abby Maitland told Maddie after her six-week checkup. "You have a clean bill of health physically."

Maddie smiled as she sat up on the table. "Are you quietly making an observation about my mental health?"

Abby shook her head. "You're doing fine." She picked up a pen, wrote some notes on a chart and closed it. Then she turned back to face Maddie. "Why don't you get dressed? I'll be back in to chat with you."

"All right." Maddie watched as Abby left the examining room. Vague unease prickled her, but Abby was so thorough, so caring as a physician. Likely the comment only unnerved Maddie because she was feeling torn about last night's realization that she and Sam were farther apart than ever.

She dressed quickly, eager to hear what Abby had to say. When the knock on the door came, she was ready. "Come in."

Abby walked into the small room bearing a cup of tea for Maddie. "It's sweet, but one of our nurses brings it from home, and if you've never had her peach tea, I think you'll find it refreshing.''

Maddie tasted it. ''It is delicious. I have to say, though, that I feel as if you're offering me some comforting tea in case I need some bracing.''

Abby shook her head. ''There is something I need to discuss with you.''

''About my mental health?''

Abby laughed. ''That came out awkward. No, you seem fine to me, Maddie. In the past several weeks when I've checked on you or seen you at Maitland, you've seemed no more stressed than any other new mother. And new wife, I might add.''

''I never thought about it that way, but I suppose I am a bit of a new wife,'' Maddie said thoughtfully.

''It's tough to adjust to each other after living apart so long. There's a comfort level to be found, one that's different from the old one before the separation, and sometimes the new rhythm can be hard to learn. Add in twins, unexpected on Sam's part, and the rhythm most likely can be a bit bouncy. I kept waiting for you to call me with a major case of baby blues, but you came through the first six weeks with flying colors. Maybe having Sam around helped.''

''I do feel blue occasionally, but Sam makes me sleep whenever I get weepy. Or he does something kind, like run out and buy a watermelon, which he splits up into small chunks and puts in the fridge so all I have to do is go fill a bowl and eat it.'' Maddie smiled. ''If I even have to do that. Usually, he's already brought it to me.''

''Good nutrition is important. As is having a support system.'' Abby smiled. ''It's a wonder you two have managed to give your recuperation the full six weeks. Some couples can't stand it and go ahead—''

''Oh, no. I might have sneaked a couple of days off the time frame, but Sam absolutely wouldn't after you gave him his orders. Not that we haven't been in bed together. We've slept together, we've jumped on the bed together. We've done everything but have sexual intercourse.''

''Good Sam.'' Abby looked pensive for a moment. ''I'm glad you have Sam to love you, Maddie. I want you to think about how much he must love you to be so caring.''

''He's very caring,'' she whispered.

''I sensed that.'' Abby took a deep breath. ''And you two are satisfied with the two children you have, and the family that you're building.''

''Well, it's been a miracle of course, but I'd be lying if I didn't admit I'm hoping for at least one more child.''

''I understand. Maddie, on that topic, Mitchell Maitland asked me to talk to you about something.''

The unease she'd felt a moment ago returned, though Abby's smile was kind and soft. ''Okay.''

''The procedure Maitland was able to perform successfully for you isn't one that could be replicated in your case.''

Alarm jumped full-force into Maddie's being at the doctor's careful choice of words. ''What are you saying exactly?''

Abby reached out to put a hand on hers. ''Dr. Maitland would not perform the same operation on you a second time. It is his medical opinion that the risks in it would be greater than the possible positive outcome. I hope that this won't disappoint you too much, Maddie. Indeed, I don't even know if you'd considered the Maitland Maternity clinic in your future plans for pregnancy—"

"Of course I had! How else would I become pregnant?" Panic pressed at Maddie from all directions.

"Then this is what Mitchell wanted you to know, so that you could plan accordingly. I know you're upset about it, but he really feels that with the successful birth of healthy, viable twins, to try the same procedure again is risking too much. You have Hayden, Henry and Sam to love, Maddie," she said softly, handing her a tissue.

Stunned, Maddie took it, clutching the tissue in her lap as tears of astonishment streaked down her cheeks. "How else would I have another baby?" she said, repeating the same question she'd asked a moment ago.

"There's always the possibility you and Sam don't need any help," Abby said gently. "It's something no one can predict."

Maddie bowed her head. "Thank you for telling me, Abby. I've been thinking that I had the safety net of Maitland whenever I wanted it. I'm glad I know." She took a deep breath, wiping her nose, feeling her chest shudder with emotion. "I wouldn't have wanted to go six or seven months thinking getting pregnant again was as simple as placing a call to Dr. Maitland. I'd rather deal with the truth."

Abby patted her shoulder. "Maybe you and Sam can concentrate on your marriage, and the family you have."

Maddie smiled through her tears. "Our babies sure

bring a lot of happiness to us. Maitland did so much for us.''

"Good.'' Abby rose and walked to the door. "You take as long as you need to compose yourself. If you need me, or have any questions, please don't hesitate to call me. I'm always available for you, Maddie.''

"I know. Thank you.'' She forced a smile to her face, though it felt like lifting stone to do it. "Abby,'' she said suddenly, "why did Mitchell tell you to talk to me about this?''

"Sam mentioned it to him in the hospital, I believe, the day you were having the photo session with Megan. I suppose Sam said something to the effect that you two were hoping to build on your family. Of course, Mitchell felt the two of you should be made aware that the limitations for the clinic's assistance in that matter had been reached, so you wouldn't get your hopes too high.''

"I see.'' The small hairs on her arms rose, but Maddie told herself it was the chill of the doctor's office, not shock. Not panic. Not heartbreak.

"Naturally, Mitchell didn't want to draw you aside and talk to you about the situation that day, Maddie. So he asked me to feel you out on the subject, and if in fact you were considering Maitland in assisting a future pregnancy, to let you know where you stood.'' Abby smiled at her brightly. "From where you're standing, it looks to me like a brand-new future for you and Sam. A rebirth of your marriage, with a bright promise of many years of happiness with those babies.''

Shrill agony streaked through Maddie. "Yes, it does look that way.''

"Remember you can call me anytime, Maddie."

"Yes. Thank you, Abby."

The doctor smiled and went out, closing the door behind her. Instantly, Maddie put her face in her hands and wept.

Sam had mentioned having more children to Mitchell Maitland.

She could not have another baby. It was a wall of finality, a dream lost. Most likely a period of her life passed by, like foam ebbing at the edge of the sea.

No, that wasn't right. She'd known the joy of childbirth. The heavenly, miraculous experience of carrying a child inside her had not passed her by. She was no dry, unfulfilled husk. This joy had been hers.

I did not share it with Sam.

During her pregnancy, in the back of her mind, she must have thought that Maitland could work one more miracle for her. Or maybe she'd simply been too selfish to share with Sam, too afraid of his reaction to what she'd done. Her chest ached with the pain, feeling almost concave, like a hollow shell.

How could she share her heartache with him, considering his recent bout of angina? *Sam, I can't have any more children. We can't have any more children.*

She closed off her sadness, though she felt as if her heart had never hurt so much. Emptiness filled her. Strangling the thought that their family wasn't quite complete without the little girl she'd dreamed of, Maddie forced herself to focus on Sam. He was supposed to rest and cut down on stress.

This news would upset him, for her sake. For her sake. With Sam, it was always for her sake.

No way would she risk setting off another attack like the one he'd suffered the other day.

"YOU'RE AWAKE," Maddie said as she walked into the kitchen. Sam sat at the table, eating breakfast and wearing only boxer shorts. Her gaze roved over him quickly, but wistfully. The two babies lay on a blanket nearby. "I was hoping all three of my men would be snoozing."

"Believe me, the boys and I had a great morning. We just got up and decided o.j. and cereal sounded like an eye-opener. For Dad, anyway. They had a bottle, which they seemed to like just fine because they pooped out right after playing with their fingers for about thirty minutes." He grinned at her. "So…are we on for a bottle of wine and some long-awaited lovemaking tonight? Not that I'm, you know—" he lowered his voice to a whisper in deference to his sons' tender ears, in case they might be listening in their sleep "—that adjective that rhymes with corny or anything."

She laughed as she set her purse down.

Sam came up behind her, scooping his hands around her bottom before holding her close against him. "How was the doctor visit?" he whispered in her ear, nuzzling her nape.

Instant fire poured into her veins. "Everything is just fine."

He turned her to face him. "Fine for tonight?"

Slowly, she allowed her gaze to move from his broad chest down his tapered stomach—with the love handles he swore were there but she couldn't see—

to a major rise in his boxer shorts. "Can you…wait that long?" she asked, meeting his eyes deliberately.

"Can you?"

She gave him a foxy look. "I've been known to like early morning lovemaking."

His eyes blazed with passion she remembered. She trailed a hand over his chest and down his stomach, to just above his waistband. "As a matter of fact, you've been known to be very virile in the a.m."

"Beautiful lady, I can be virile at any hour of the day just by looking at your sweet body."

She tapped his lip with a finger. "Impressive boasting."

"Uh-uh. Impressive track record." He kissed her neck, down along her collarbone, and slipped his hands up under her breasts. "Did the doctor give you the green light?"

"Maybe a yellow."

He stopped kissing her to stare worriedly into her eyes. "Yellow?"

"Green to go, but yellow to proceed with caution," she said, slipping her own hands inside his boxers so that she could feel his buttocks. "There may be some tightness at first since I had an episiotomy, which might be uncomfortable. In other words, go slow."

He unzipped her sundress, letting it drop to the kitchen floor. She stepped out of her sandals. Gently, he unclasped her bra, taking her enlarged breasts in his hands. "You're beautiful," he said huskily. He bent to kiss each breast, tasting the nipples with his mouth before teasing them into hard puckers. She moaned, her hands reaching for his head to hold him closer to her. He licked her slowly as his hands moved down to slide into her panties.

She gasped from the feel of him cupping her mound. He pushed down her panties and she stepped out of them. "I'd forgotten how wet you make me," she said breathlessly.

"I'd forgotten how hard you make me. I feel like I'm going to explode. But," he told her, "I'm proceeding with caution. Doctor's orders."

He lifted her, carrying her to the sofa, which was on the opposite side of the baby blankets. "Privacy, first thing."

"Definitely," she agreed. "Second thing, let me remove those boxers for you. They seem to be in the way."

"Not anymore." He shoved them down, revealing stark evidence of his desire for her.

Maddie looked up at Sam with glowing eyes.

"Lie back," he told her, pushing her gently into the pillows of the overstuffed sofa as he lay beside her. They stared into each other's eyes. "I've missed you for far too long to rush this." He slid a finger along her heat as he sealed his mouth to hers, kissing and sucking at her lips as he stroked her below. "I always liked how eager you get for me," he murmured after a moment.

"Sam," she moaned. She could feel his hard strength against her leg, and she wanted to feel it inside her.

"Not yet." He pressed kisses to her lips. "I've missed your mouth. I've missed you kissing me. Kiss me, Maddie."

She did, and he slid his finger inside her. She

nearly fainted with the surprising pleasure of it. He caught her gasp of excitement in his mouth, sucking until she felt her breath might leave her. When he moved to kiss her chin, she strained up against him, but he said, "Relax. I'm not going to rush this. Remember, go slowly."

"Not this slowly! I think I'm going to cry if you don't get inside me," she said frantically, taking him into her hands so that she could stroke him to the same fever pitch burning her.

He moved a second finger inside her, gently enlarging her, and Maddie moaned. "Please, Sam," she begged.

"I want to please you. I'm going to please you. Relax." He bent his head to lick at her nipples again, moving up over her so that he was poised at her entrance. Maddie reached for his hips to draw him into her, but he shook his head. "No. Let me do this."

She groaned as he moved slightly inside her, his finger moving to caress the delicate skin just above. Tremors began to build inside her as he gently stroked back and forth, back and forth, just an inch inside her, letting her get used to the feel of him so there would be no pain.

"Sam," she said, suddenly swept up on a wave of intense longing, "Sam, don't stop. Don't stop— oh, my—"

"Go, Maddie," he encouraged her. "Let go. I want to feel you this way."

Closing her eyes, she let herself feel the wave of cresting climax, grabbing at his shoulders so she could force him into her, but he held back until she felt the release. Then, when she thought the joy couldn't get any more intense, he began moving deeper and deeper in the same back and forth motion until he was finally completely joined with her.

"Are you all right?" he asked, his voice raspy against her neck.

"I'm better than all right." She wrapped her legs around his waist. "I want more. Take me, Sam. Do it. You're not going to hurt me."

He groaned, and she smiled, liking the passion she made him feel. Now that he was certain she wasn't going to be hurt by him, he pumped more ardently, rocking her with the sensation she wanted so badly. Her nipples hardened again as she held on tightly to him, keeping herself clasped against him so he could find the pleasure she wanted to give him.

"Maddie," he said between clenched teeth. "Maddie—I never want to be without you again," he growled, throwing his head back as the climax rolled through his body. She could feel it resonating inside her like thunder.

He collapsed against her, his back sweat soaked, his breathing hard. After a moment, they moved so they could snuggle against each other. Sam reached to pull an afghan over her as he kissed her. "That was just what the doctor ordered."

"Sam!" But she laughed, and as they fell asleep, wrapped in each others arms, she didn't let herself think about what Abby had told her.

AFTER THE WONDERFULLY blissful morning they shared, there was no telling Sam what she'd learned.

It wasn't fair to burden him. Maddie wanted to make him happy, chase the stress away.

When she felt blues pressing on her, she went into the master bathroom and sat, staring at the fountain. The beautiful woman wore a long gown, exposing a bare leg as she poured water into a basin. It was an exquisite statue, and Maddie loved looking at it.

Even if it did spit instead of flow, it was a lovely image of womanhood. Maddie liked the rocks in the basin, the permanence below the crystal water. Water was a sign of life. She loved dipping her fingers into it, watching the ripples as she touched it.

"You are a treasure," she told the statue. "I guess you know you seem perfect except for your obvious flaw."

Sam came into the bathroom at that moment, seeing her looking at the fountain. "The boys are in their cribs. I was going to take a shower, unless you were about to…."

She shook her head. "No. Not yet." She planned to bathe eventually and change into some stretchy shorts.

He came up behind her to press his face against her neck. "That statue freaks me out."

Maddie smiled. "I don't even notice her plumbing problem anymore."

"I do." He stepped around Maddie, leaning to look at the back and the underside of the basin. "I can't figure out what our mothers did wrong. It looks to me like they did everything just right."

Maddie smacked his hand lightly. "Leave my statue alone, please. She doesn't need to be fixed."

He gave her a hurt look, which was so fake Maddie shook her head at him.

"I could fix her."

"Leave her just the way she is, please."

"Let me take her back to the store and get one that works properly."

"Absolutely not!" Maddie was horrified. "She has a tiny defect. That doesn't make her...less special."

"No, it doesn't. It means she needs to be stamped 'return to vendor' so she can be replaced."

Chills swept Maddie's arms. "But she's mine, and I like her just the way she is. She's a gift from our mothers. I wouldn't dream of taking her back."

He shook his head. "Suit yourself. Let me know if you change your mind." Stripping off his shirt, he said, "By the way, Maddie, while we're on the subject of gifts, I was wondering where your wedding band is."

Chapter Sixteen

Sam knew from the suddenly wary look in Maddie's eyes that he wasn't going to like what he was about to hear. She stared at him, her jade eyes wide with discomfort. Her full lips trembled ever so slightly.

So he waited for her to tell him. Maybe she would simply say that her hands were too swollen from the pregnancy to wear them. He would take them to a jeweler and get the band and the engagement ring resized at once.

"I sold them back to the jeweler we bought them from," she said softly, "to pay for the operation."

His jaw dropped. He'd never thought about the cost she'd incurred in the risky procedure she'd undergone. "Maddie Winston! How could you?"

"I did it in a heartbeat," she stated firmly, "and I would do it again. The bills came after you'd moved to France, and I wasn't about to call and ask you for money, Sam."

"That's not what I mean! How could you not...I mean, why wouldn't you call and tell me...never mind." He sank onto the edge of the tub, staring at her. "Maddie." Dumbstruck, he shook his head.

She knit her lips together. "I'm sorry."

He sighed. "I'm not upset about you selling the rings. I can replace them in a heartbeat. But Maddie, it tears me up to think that you might have needed things and wouldn't tell me. I can't stand the thought of it."

"You'd been very generous financially, Sam. You couldn't possibly have known that I wanted expensive medical procedures. Not covered by insurance, I might add. I didn't quite mortgage the house to get those babies, but—"

He swept her into his lap. They slid to the carpet from the tub, and he held her, rocking her in his arms. He kissed her forehead tenderly, telling her with his actions that he didn't care about money as much as he cared about her.

And then, for some reason he couldn't explain, he cried. Silently, she wiped his tears with her fingers, until his cheeks were dry.

"YOU KNOW, I wonder if it's unhealthy for the babies to sleep in bed with us," Maddie remarked as the four of them stayed up for late-night TV.

Sam admired Maddie's long, bare legs, exposed by the thigh-length T-shirt she wore. Damn it, a T-shirt shouldn't be sexy, but his woman's legs were so fine it was all he could do not to grab her by the ankles and feast his way up. He reached for the popcorn in the bowl between them, situated where the babies couldn't reach in accidentally.

"The family that watches reruns of *Dick van Dyke* and *The Courtship of Eddie's Father,* as well as a healthy dose of British comedies, stays together," he

said, still thinking about her as he ate the popcorn.
Idly, he wondered if she wore any panties under the
T-shirt. Probably, but that was a problem he could
quickly fix. Much easier than the other issues they
were tackling.

"No, it's the family that ends up with the same
taste in TV programming," Maddie said sensibly.

"I'm sure there's a psychologist out there who
would tell you that the boys shouldn't be in bed with
us, and your mother probably told you a hundred
times not to eat in bed. It's so much more fun to just
relax, though, isn't it?"

"Yeah." She smiled at him. "Why do I feel like
we're on our own little vacation?"

"You gave up breast-feeding, which took you off
the soft-serve, short-order schedule."

She nodded. "I feel a little guilty—"

"Don't. I was a bottle baby, and I turned out to
be a great, strapping hunk. Or close enough." He
tossed some popcorn into his mouth and reached for
the glass of soda on the nightstand. "There must be
ninety-five percent guilt in parenting and five percent
heck-yeah-I'm-right-on. I think we should resolve
that, no matter what, we build each other up. There's
an awful lot of negativity out there you women have
to deal with. I was watching one of those talk shows
today while you were in the shower—"

"You were not!"

"I was. The boys were hungry, so I flipped on the
TV as I gave them their bottles. Children need this,
children need that...hey, nobody knows what children need. I say parents need to be with their children, and that's the end of what needs to be heard

from the wisenheimers. A close family is like a strong backbone—it holds everything together.''

"Sam Winston," Maddie declared, "you sound like my mother."

"Well, maybe just once she was right." He rolled his head on the pillow to look at her. "I always knew you'd be a good mother. Even if you do get popcorn salt in the sheets."

She threw an unpopped kernel at him. "You get laundry duty tomorrow."

"I don't mind laundry duty. I do mind you not having a wedding band."

He stared at her purposefully. His heart beat harder as he waited for her reply to that.

She said nothing.

They both went back to pretending they were watching TV.

"Tell me what I'm not doing right," Sam said after a moment. "I'll fix it."

"It's not you," she said. "It's me. And you can't fix me. I can't even fix me."

"I like you just the way you are."

"I have a lot to think about," she said softly. "And I don't want to rush it."

"I do understand, Maddie." He winced. "It's just so hard feeling left out. I don't know if you want romance, or a new wedding ring, or—"

"I want time, Sam. Time to figure out what I'm doing. And to think about how I fit with you."

"Last I noticed, we fit together just fine," he grumbled.

"If you don't stop gnashing your teeth, you're going to start up your chest pain again."

"Maddie!" Sam roared. "Don't baby me!"

Startled, the babies began to cry.

"Oh, for heaven's sake, Sam." Maddie got up from the bed, hurrying to wash her hands so that she could pick up Hayden. Sam bundled Henry to his chest. After a few moments, they were able to calm the infants.

Maddie eyed him then, highly disgruntled. "Sam. I have some things on my mind I told you I wanted to deal with for a while. I don't think I'm asking for a whole lot. If you don't bug me about…you know, exerting total control over this relationship, I promise not to badger you about your heart. Okay?"

He frowned. "Is that what you think? That I'm trying to exert control over you?"

"I think you're being a bit heavy-handed. We're sleeping together. We're under the same roof. We're parenting our children together. Do we have to be locked at the neck for you to feel satisfied?"

His brows raised. "Would you care to tell me exactly what's bothering you, sweetheart?"

Her shoulders sagged instantly. "Abby told me today that Mitchell Maitland can't do another procedure for me. Actually that Maitland wouldn't advise doing the same procedure twice."

She held her baby, staring at Sam with dismay. Sam could feel his heart bleeding for his wife as surely as if someone had opened his chest and taken a knife to it. "I'm sorry, Maddie."

"I don't want to be at the end of my childbearing, Sam. I'm not trying to be selfish or ungrateful. It's just that—" she glanced down at Henry for a moment before catching her breath again "—it's just that I loved feeling…whole. I loved being pregnant. I felt like Mother Earth in full spring bloom.'' She sank to the edge of the bed, laying her quieted baby back on the blanket. ''I thought this time you and I could go through a pregnancy together. But I was wrong. And I didn't want to tell you because I didn't want to burden you with my problems, but…''

He wanted to cry again when he heard her voice breaking. He understood now why she'd asked for time. It really wasn't him. He'd prefer it if she wasn't pushing him away, but he understood that, too. He had done the same thing when he'd suffered his angina attack. ''Maddie, I have to be honest about something.''

She turned to face him. ''What?''

''I'm not proud of this, but I already knew. I couldn't tell you. I'm sorry. It was a lousy, chicken-hearted thing to do, because I could have comforted you. You could have come to me instead of suffering by yourself. And I hope you can forgive me.''

He got up from the bed and walked to her side, hunkering between her knees. ''I knew you'd be crushed. And I guess I wanted to spare both of us as long as possible. Never did I dream Dr. Abby would tell you. I thought you'd mention making an appointment at Maitland one day, and then I'd…'' He shook his head. ''I don't know. Somehow find the words to tell you.''

She took a gasp of air. ''I found out in a doctor's office, Sam. You could have saved me that.''

''I'm so sorry. It was lame. I have no excuse except that I didn't think it would come up today. And even so, I thought I'd take you to your checkup, as I did last time.''

"Yes, you did." Maddie pushed her soft brown hair behind her ear and looked at him. "Sam, I need time. Everything inside me is jumbled up and turned inside out. I don't know that I have one thought that stays on track before it hits another thought and gets turned around. I'm not suffering from postpartum, and I'm not losing my mind, but...I need some space to myself."

He swallowed painfully. "Do you want me to move back next door?"

She hesitated so long he thought he could hear minutes ticking by in his head.

"I don't think so," she whispered. "Just don't keep mentioning wedding rings and marriage to me. Let me get my soul reconnected to my spirit."

It was so hard to say yes, to give her that time, when all he wanted to do was crush her to him and tell her that he would protect her, would keep her safe. If he had to, he would pick up the minute fragments of her broken heart and piece them all back together, sliver by sliver, if it took him a lifetime to do it.

But that wasn't what she wanted right now.

"Do you want me to sleep on the sofa? I'll do it. We can go back to swapping duties like we were."

She looked away from him, her gaze focusing on the darkness outside the sliding glass doors. "Stay," she said. "We're a family. And maybe I'll find my backbone eventually."

After a moment of staring at her pale, porcelain

face, he rose to his feet. He dropped a light kiss on her forehead, just at her hairline.

Then he got back on his side of the king-size bed.

This time, it wasn't his chest that suffered unendurable pain. It was his bones, flesh, heart, mind—his very spirit.

His soul.

She was his soul. Without her, he was only existing.

Chapter Seventeen

The following afternoon, loving disaster struck.

"We're back!" Franny called up the stairs. "Anybody home?"

Maddie glanced at Sam, surprised and a trifle alarmed. "Did you know they were returning today?"

He shook his head. "Nope."

"Up here," Maddie called. She swooped up Henry and went to greet the travelers.

The grandparents hurried upstairs, and Maddie met them at the top of the staircase. Everyone hugged, and the babies were immediately admired by the newly returned family members.

"My, they've grown!" Franny said, taking Henry from Maddie. "You're quite the little gentleman now!"

Maddie smiled proudly as Sam relinquished Hayden to Severn.

"A pair of princes," Sara said. "My goodness, I feel like we've been gone for ages! We didn't miss out on anything, did we? Did anything...exciting happen while we were away?"

Sam and Maddie shared a glance at his mother's hopeful tone.

"Not too much," she said, not wanting to talk about what she suspected they wanted to know about most—how she and Sam were getting along. "We mostly worked on settling into a routine."

It was a hedge, but it was all she had at the moment. "Did you decide not to buy a château in France?" she asked.

Everyone found something to sit on, preferably close to a baby. "We had so much fun traveling that we decided we don't want to stay in one place. We want to keep going!" Franny said, her eyes fairly twinkling with delight. "Next up is Singapore!"

"Singapore?" Sam and Maddie repeated.

"What your mother is trying to say," Virgil interjected, "is that we may be more the hobo sort. We like traveling with Sara and Severn, and we all agree there's a hundred different places we've never seen and want to. But we had to come back and see our little grandchildren before we journey to the next port."

"I'm glad that you enjoyed France," Sam said.

"We were hoping you might, too," Franny stated, adjusting the baby in her arms. "While we're recharging our batteries and making our reservations, why don't you let us keep the babies and you two go to France?"

"It seems a shame that Maddie hasn't seen Jardin," Sara agreed. "It's something else, Sam. We're very proud of you."

Cahoots. Clearly, this was a preplanned agenda to get them alone together in a setting known for romance. Maddie didn't dare look at Sam. Their parents were always trying to be so helpful—they couldn't possibly know that the last thing she and Sam would do right now was take a trip. There was absolutely no point in it.

"What about it, Maddie?" Sam asked. "Since you've quit breast-feeding, we wouldn't be upsetting the babies' routine. I'd be happy to take you to see your new wine company."

She stared at him, dismayed. How could he twist her arm in front of their parents? Once she turned him down, and the folks realized she was the sticking point, they would do everything within their power to unstick her. All in her best interests, of course.

As soon as she said no, regardless of how nicely she refused the offer, they were going to gang up on her.

"We'll talk about it another time," she said smoothly, getting to her feet to kiss each of the grandparents. "Now that Sam has some reinforcements, I think I'll take a nap."

Everyone agreed that was an excellent idea. Without meeting Sam's eyes, Maddie made her escape, hurrying to her bedroom to lock the door behind her. Taking a deep breath, she let it out heavily.

If she was going to elude their machinations until she could see them off to another continent, she was going to have to be extra vigilant. Clearly they'd come back to America with some new thoughts on "helping" her.

ALL FOUR GRANDPARENTS stared at Sam after Maddie exited the room. Their gazes could only be described as hopeful. Eager. He gave a vague smile and cleared his throat. "Nice try, all of you."

"But not quite successful." Franny eyed him. "Perhaps we didn't stay gone long enough?"

He gave up the smile and the cheery persona. "I think it's too much to expect that two weeks would solve everything that happened over the last couple of years."

Virgil nodded. "Best to have the hang-tough attitude."

"Oh, what would you know?" Franny said crossly. "Sam's been hanging tough. We've got us a stubborn daughter."

"Where's Joey?" Sam suddenly realized one in-law was missing.

"Our stubborn son is still in France enjoying himself," Franny said, even more crossly. "He's talking crazy!"

"Crazy?" Sam raised an eyebrow and glanced at his folks.

Sara sighed and filled in the details, since the Bradys seemed unable to speak of it. "He doesn't seem to have your reservations for falling head over heels and following his heart, no matter where that leads him. He's talking about settling in France for good."

"Isn't he due to report to football training camp soon? College should be starting—"

"Seems he'd rather get a degree in love," Severn interrupted. "Needless to say, Franny and Virgil are taking their son's decision with great distress."

Indeed, Franny held on to her husband with both hands as he patted her comfortingly. Sam's lips flattened. He didn't know what to say. Actually, it was none of his business—except that he sensed some pithy, appropriate comment would be well received.

He was fresh out of appropriate comfort. Maddie would know what to say. She and her brother were exceptionally close. "Maybe you should talk to Maddie," he said.

"Maddie?" Franny's voice rose. "What can she do? Joey's well and truly hooked."

"No, I mean that Maddie is probably the best person to talk to," he said helplessly. "I don't know if the situation calls for congratulations or commiserations."

"How could it call for congratulations?" Franny asked sternly.

He was stepping into a position that would likely earn him no points with his in-laws. Sam didn't want to, but there was an obvious point he couldn't ignore. "Seems to me love only comes once in some folks' lives. Maybe this is Joey's true love. And that would call for congratulations."

Franny and Virgil were outraged. "That would be fine if it was love instead of a summer romance— not worth throwing away one's whole life over," Virgil commented.

Maddie slipped into the room, putting her hand on Sam's arm. "I can hear you all bickering from my room. If you want to continue your conversation, go to a more comfortable location. I want to put the babies down for a nap."

"Your brother has fallen in love," Sam told her.

"I know. I heard the whole thing." She smiled up at him wryly. "I can tell you this debate won't be decided for several hours. Head to the kitchen and get yourselves some refreshments. I'll be right down.''

Sam hung back to help her. "Think I'll let them settle themselves for a minute.''

"That would probably be best.''

Together, they changed the babies' diapers and put their sons into their cribs, after holding them quietly for a few moments.

"They're overexcited,'' Maddie said.

"I think our parents always are.''

"I meant the babies. More stimulation than they've been used to.''

"Oh.'' Sam snorted. "Well, me, too.''

"I think I see the outline of their plan,'' Maddie told him. "The reason they want me to go rushing over to France is not so much to see the company as it is to talk sense into Joey.''

"Ahh. I didn't think of that angle.''

"I didn't either until you startled them by saying that true love may only come once, and this woman might be Joey's. They didn't like your answer, and yet they've always been huge proponents of matchmaking, fixing up relationships, and true love. Strange that they're not shaking the love beads this time.'' She frowned. "I can't think it's the football they're holding out for, although they're very proud of him, and his grades.''

"Maybe they think he's too young.''

"Maybe. But Mom and Dad married young.''

"And they've always been happy.''

"Well…'' Maddie looked hesitant as she went back to sit in a rocker. She rocked back and forth a moment, remembering. "The unexposed branch in our very shady family tree is that Mom and Dad actually…"

"Actually?" Sam couldn't wait to hear whatever it was Maddie didn't want to reveal.

She lowered her gaze for a moment. "I don't think I can tell you."

Sam was astonished. "I've known you for six years! There were times I thought I knew you better than I knew myself. What could you possibly have hidden from me?" Besides a pregnancy, but he decided this was not the moment to qualify his question.

She blushed, a becoming pink that flooded the skin around the neckline of her white-and-navy sundress. He took the rocker next to her, checking the agitated motion of her chair with his foot so she'd have to meet his gaze.

Slowly, she raised her eyelashes to look at him. The look was pure mischief. "There are some skeletons that like the darkness of the family closet."

He blinked. "I dread to think what might be hanging out in there with the cobwebs. But let's shine the light of day on it, anyway."

"I don't think I can. I've never told anyone."

"Maddie! You are not allowed to keep secrets from your husband!" he mock roared.

"Shh!" She sat up to see if the napping babies had stirred, but the bunny-blanket-covered bodies remained peaceful.

He caught her hand. "No more avoiding the truth."

A light smile played at her mouth. "Did you ever

think there were an awful lot of years between Joey and me?''

''Nineteen years isn't all that unusual,'' he said, avoiding the point. ''Joey was a late-in-life baby.''

''That's what everyone supposes. The truth is,'' she said, taking a deep breath and giving him a cagey look, ''is that Mom and Dad weren't married when they found out I was on the way.''

Sam's eyebrow slid upward. ''Imagine that. Unprotected passion in the fifties.'' He grimaced. ''Why do I have trouble imagining Franny and Virgil as randy teenagers?''

''They were planning on getting married,'' Maddie said hurriedly. ''But they were very young, and their parents objected.''

''How young?''

''Sixteen. Which wasn't terribly young back then, truly, but Mom's parents wanted her to get a college education, and so did Dad's. They didn't want them to sweat out life on farms the way they had. My grandparents were tough pioneer stock who had always lived in the country and never had any luxuries.'' She sighed heavily. ''So their parents wanted more for their children. All parents do. But Dad met Mom at a church social and it was love at first sight, and a little bit more than was considered proper at the time.''

''Particularly at a church social!''

''No!'' Maddie laughed, tapping his wrist to make him pay attention.

Of its own accord, it seemed, his hand covered hers and lingered. She didn't pull away, and Sam liked the feeling of the two of them sitting together, so he hoped she wouldn't notice what he was up to.

"They didn't fall that fast, but it was fast enough that I was pretty much a fact by the next time the preacher came to town. Mom and Dad were married quickly and quietly. No fuss, no parties, no nothing." Maddie leaned her head back on the rocker before turning to make certain Sam was listening.

He most certainly was. "Go on."

"Well, it might have been love at first sight, but even love can flicker when a family is poor and young and can't make ends meet. They started wondering what might have happened had they gotten those college educations, and my grandparents were there to encourage them to give it a try."

"Really? That was supportive."

"Not exactly. They would send only one of them. And college was very far from small towns back then. A bus ride and a train ride, at least."

"But your father was trying to make a better way for his family."

"They sent my mother. It was her parents who offered to help out."

"But they weren't really helping at all, then."

"No. They wanted her to see what she'd missed out on by getting married young and having a baby. They wanted her to find a man who could give her more than poverty and a farm that faced ruin almost every year."

Now Maddie's fingers curled into his. Sam welcomed the closeness.

"My father couldn't handle being alone. He didn't like her parents raising me, and he felt left out. The story he'd been given was that he needed to stay behind and take care of the farm, but after a while, he figured it out. And he was hurt that Mom had left him.''

''Did she go back to him?''

Maddie shook her head. ''He gave her an ultimatum—come home or we get a divorce. By then, Mom was deep into her third quarter and realized she had a talent for learning. She was smart and quick thinking, and she'd decided to become a trained nurse. Dad said she could be a nurse for any local doctor near the cotton farm, but by then she wanted to see what else she could do. I know that sounds selfish, but Mom had never done anything for herself. She'd been manipulated by her parents into being a small-town beauty queen, their shining diamond out in the sticks. She was a dutiful daughter. Falling in love with my dad was her first rebellion. Finding out she could make it at college and wanting to stick it out was her second. It was a different world for women then.''

Sam didn't say anything, but he couldn't help thinking how fortunate he was that his parents had known they wanted each other for good when he was born.

He also decided that any ultimatum issued to a Brady woman probably didn't turn out best for the male involved. He'd given Maddie one of his own and found himself alone in France, cooling his heels. Fortunately, he'd had a compelling reason to return, or he'd still be over there, trying to convince himself he was happy.

He had not been happy without her.

"So they divorced." Maddie shrugged, as if it didn't matter, but he knew it must have hurt her terribly if she'd kept it hidden from him. "Mom went on to get her degree, and Dad kept the farm. I rotated among the three households, and I guess I resented it. I couldn't understand why other kids had normal families and I didn't have a sibling, or parents under one roof. They stayed apart for six years," Maddie said softly. "I know, because on my sixth birthday, neither of my parents made it to my birthday. My mother's train was stuck in Dallas, and my father's cotton crop had been hit by boll weevils. He had no money for a ticket. I wouldn't blow out the birthday candles on the lovely cake my grandparents had made me until my parents came and watched me." She slipped him a glance. "I sat and waited, until I finally fell asleep by my beautiful cake. It was pink and white, and had Happy Birthday, Maddie written on it."

"Oh, Maddie." Sam pulled her into his arms, edging her around on the rocker so he could hold her close. "That breaks my heart."

"Apparently, it broke my grandparents', too, because they decided their meddling had backfired. They bought bus tickets for my mom and my dad to come, and they were there in two days, in time for a slightly stale cake. A small talk with my grandparents convinced my parents that the family needed to be together—and then Grandma and Grandpa stayed out of my parents' decision. They said they'd support them no matter what they wanted." Maddie smiled at her husband. "Mom and I went home with Dad, and it was the best birthday I ever had."

"I'm so glad this story had a happy ending." He nuzzled her neck, wondering if theirs was going to have one, too.

"Me, too. Mom's education paid off and she got a good job in town. Dad's cotton never did do that well, until one day Mom decided she'd be better off staying home and doctoring him and the plants instead of patients. They resolved never to meddle in my life, except with good intentions."

Sam and Maddie shared a grin.

"Ah, the road to hell is paved with good intentions," he said wryly.

"Exactly. I think that's why they went to France, initially."

"Far, far away from temptation."

"Yes. And they'd never traveled anywhere together. I think they'll always be conscious of the years they lost. And though they grew a lot when they were apart, and ultimately found their way back to each other, that separation is always at the back of their minds. It makes them take very good care of each other."

Sam squeezed her fingers lightly. His separation from Maddie had been hellish—mainly because he had known it was over between them. The pain of still wanting her was something he'd thought would ease in time.

It had not diminished, instead growing worse. That was a period of his life he didn't want to revisit. "So, about Joey," he prompted.

"Well, Joey was an unexpected blessing they never thought they'd see. I suppose after the years of separation, they thought their childlessness was a sort of penance.''

He remembered that ache very well, too.

"There I was, going off to college. And my mom was pregnant." A soft, whimsical smile lit Maddie's face as she looked at him. "Do you realize my parents were younger when they had Joey than I was when I became pregnant?"

"Let's not talk like that," he said gruffly. "I don't want to think about it."

"It means we don't have nineteen years of child-bearing for lightning to strike," she murmured.

"It means," Sam said decisively, "that we better not linger too long over our mistakes."

They stared at each other. Maddie's eyes were wide as she took in what he'd said.

"I'm serious," he insisted huskily. "If the second time is the charm, as your mother seems to believe, I want to start rubbing the rabbit's foot now."

Maddie looked away for an instant. "I don't think I ever looked at it like that."

He used her fingers, which were still entwined with his, to tap his chest. "If they can do it, so can we. Right?"

"It sounds reasonable," she said slowly, her thoughts somewhere far away. "I suppose they're good role models."

"Maybe in a sense. But we have to blaze our own trail."

"You just don't want to identify with my parents."

"I don't want to identify that much with mine," Sam admitted. "However, this whole thing makes sense now. Your parents aren't happy about Joey blowing what they see as his big chance. They don't want to interfere, in case this is the love of his life. So they want to send you in, hoping you'll be able to steer Joey back onto the right path.''

"The notion does make a certain amount of sense," Maddie said with a sigh. "Joey's very young, and they would remember their indiscreet love. No doubt they're panicking at the very thought of another pregnancy—"

"Maddie!" Franny softly called up the stairs.

Sam stared at Maddie. "Why did that sound a little desperate?"

"She's your mother-in-law. You've learned to read her pretty well." Maddie rose, crossing to the stairwell to peer down. "Yes?"

"I was wondering if the babies are asleep, if maybe we could have a family caucus."

"Sure." She glanced over her shoulder at Sam. "Family caucus time. You remember those, don't you?"

"Last time your family called one in which I was included it was to discuss what Aunt Berol should be buried in, funeral parlor clothes or something of her own, since she was a notorious tightwad."

"Shh!" Maddie shushed him, not wanting to get her mother started on that subject all over again. "She wasn't a tightwad, she was frugal. During the Depression, it was a learned survival tactic. She learned it well."

Sam took Maddie's hand as he came to the stairwell. "I promise that, no matter what, I won't say a

word during this caucus. No matter how your mother
tries to draw me in.''

"It would have helped if you hadn't decided to
play devil's advocate over Aunt Berol's attire,"
Maddie grumbled. "Mother wasn't used to thinking
with logic instead of sentiment. As far as she was
concerned, Aunt Berol never parted with a penny in
her life so why should she start in death?''

Kissing Maddie's hand, Sam said, "This time you
and I stand together. Think of me as your secret
weapon. Whatever you say goes. Period.''

"No matter what?''

He stared down at her. "If I make so much as a
contrary peep, I'll pay you back in service. I'll stay
up with the babies. I'll rub your feet. Or buy tickets
for your parents to fly to Singapore.''

She raised her brow. "I love my parents.''

"I know you do. So do I.''

He guided her down the stairs, reassuring himself
that everyone in this house had learned from their
past mistakes. This family caucus would be a bond-
ing, democratic, decision-making process—without
any input from him that his wife didn't want.

Chapter Eighteen

Maddie warily approached the family members seated around the kitchen table. Severn and Sara were sitting across from her parents. She knew the subject had to be about Joey.

Of course, she wasn't going to France. There was no way she would leave Sam at this critical juncture. That was something she had learned from her parents.

One separation was enough.

Joey's life was his own. She knew enough about minding one's own business not to dabble in anyone else's.

"You asked us to keep an eye on the family business while we were in France," Sara began when everyone was seated.

Maddie perked up. This topic was unexpected.

"Well, yes," Sam hesitantly agreed, knowing that it had been a ruse he'd cooked up to get their parents out of their hair for a while. Maddie smiled at him reassuringly. They would play along.

"We have reason to believe matters are not going as you would wish," Severn said.

"Oh?" Sam raised a brow.

"We think the books are being cooked," Franny said without further skirting. "We think Vivi may have married Martin to keep you from being suspicious of what she and her brother, Jean-Luc, were up to with Jardin."

Maddie's eyes widened. "Martin is Sam's best friend."

"Exactly. The perfect foil," Virgil said. "The stooge. The lovestruck schnook. Maybe even the fall guy," he finished dramatically.

"Dad!" Maddie exclaimed. "You don't believe we're going to buy this, do you? I mean, Mom, you never stop trying to make things work, even though you try to mind your own business. But you, Dad. Honestly, I'm ashamed." She shook her head at her father. "I thought everyone understood that Sam and I have to do this without you trying to push us together."

He didn't wither under her censure. "I know what I saw," he insisted. "There are shipments that aren't accounted for. Payroll that isn't being recorded properly. I know I'm just a cotton farmer," he said, his tone belligerent as his brows drew together, "but one thing I know is books. They gotta be kept just so, or there's unaccounted shortages and overages that end up as a loss in someone's pocket. Yours," he said to Sam. "Because you think Martin's going to keep everything kosher for you. What are best friends for, anyway?"

"But you're here, Son," Severn said. "We may be crazy, but we think you'd best go take a look."

Sam scratched at his chin. Maddie's lips were

parted. She didn't know what to say. Her parents had never recommended a separation, never encouraged them to be apart. In fact, they had gone embarrassingly overboard to shove them into each other's arms.

Why would they now—unless they really believed there was a problem?

Sam didn't say a word. He seemed puzzled and concerned. But mostly, he seemed to be waiting for her to speak.

She blinked at him, wondering why he didn't say anything.

And then she realized he had promised to support her, no matter what. His silence was loud and clear. Whatever she wanted, he would do.

But that's when I thought this was all about Joey! she wanted to cry. She had been determined not to be separated from Sam; she had wanted to spend time with him and their babies.

After what she'd just told him about her parents, he might not feel comfortable saying he would leave. She swallowed. ''Sam, you have to do what's best for Jardin.''

''I have to do what's best for you,'' he replied. ''For our family.''

''Can we have a moment?'' she asked the assembled family.

They all got up and filed out silently.

''I get the terrible feeling they're not bluffing,'' Maddie said quietly.

''So do I. This time, they're serious.''

''They wouldn't want you to leave me right now—not while they want so badly for us to work out our marriage—unless there was truly a problem. I think they're upset about Joey, but it's more than that." She reached out and took his fingers in hers. "Sam, we have plenty of time to work out our situation."

"It's not a situation. It's our marriage, and no company is worth forfeiting this time with my family. We know this is only going to happen for us once. I'm not going to blow it by not being here."

"I love the way you talk to me," she said, pressing her lips to his fingers. "You became very adept at romance after your trip to France."

He frowned. "I became very adept at romance after I discovered my wife had two babies and I was missing out on everything that mattered." Clearing his throat, he said, "I will always romance you, Maddie."

"I'll let you," she said softly. "Let's go to our room and further discuss this unexpected dilemma."

"From every angle," he confirmed.

"I want you to know that no matter what you decide, I'll support you," she said as he took her hand to lead her down the hall toward their room. "Sam, I honestly want you to do whatever you need to. This is important."

He closed the bedroom door behind them. "This is important," he said, kissing her lips.

"And this is important," she said, returning his kiss.

"And this is just as necessary." He pressed gentle kisses along her shoulders.

"And I find that this part of you demands my utmost attention." She glided her fingers along his shoulders, to his chest, where she enjoyed the tight muscles under his skin.

"And these," he said huskily, kissing down her breasts toward her nipples, "are of paramount importance." He licked each one, then suckled more intently.

She gasped, feeling flames of desire light within her. Fast-burning tinder caught fire in her nerve endings and streaked to her feminine core. "Sam," she said weakly. She wrapped her fingers in his hair. "You're beyond important," she added desperately as he kissed down her stomach, squeezing her buttocks with his hands. "You're everything to me," she cried, as he parted her with his tongue, claiming her with a fiery slickness she craved.

He licked and laved her, pushing in so that nothing escaped him, before withdrawing lightly to tease her sensitive pearl. Maddie shivered, her heart thundering, her soul on fire. It was happening fast, and faster still, as his attention brought her to a peak on which she balanced treacherously. He sensed her need for release and plunged his tongue deeper, drawing an agonized moan from her. Just when she thought she might scream from the pressure building inside her, he pressed her buttocks together, rapidly sliding in and out with his tongue, finally flicking the tip of her diamond-hard passion. She cried out his name as she climaxed, and he rose, impaling her so swiftly that she barely felt the emptiness before he filled her again.

Rocking back toward the bed, they fell onto it, mindless with desire to be one with each other. They came together in heart-stopping, desperate thrusts, reaching for the one thing they both wanted. And when they found it, they clung to each other as the waves rolled over them, bringing them to shore.

Their marriage.

It doesn't have to be just a memory, Maddie told herself as she held Sam to her pounding heart.

It could be forever.

"You have to go," she whispered in his ear as he lay over her, their bodies entwined on the wide bed.

"I don't want to leave you. Come with me."

"The babies…" she reminded him worriedly.

"Will be better off if we're together."

Her eyes widened. He had a point.

"You scared the hell out of me with that tale about your parents. We've already had one separation, and it was too damned long for me. Come with me."

"It seems selfish to Henry and Hayden."

"Support me," he told her.

"I do," she replied. "Book the flight."

IN THE END, Maddie knew she had to be with Sam. If they were ever going to learn to lean on each other, it would be better to be with him. The babies were too young to travel, she thought, so she would leave them with four doting grandparents.

It was one of the hardest things she'd ever done.

But her time with Sam had taught her something: she'd focused on the process of having children, and not the goal of building a life with her husband.

She wasn't going to make the same mistake twice. She had to love him better, more completely. She couldn't control her body's timetable for having children, but she was in control of her own decisions.

And her decision was to reprioritize.

She needed to make her marriage work. Consequently, if Sam wanted her, she would be at his side.

"I know you'll be busy, but please check on Joey," Franny pleaded as they boarded the plane. "Try to make him see sense."

Maddie smiled and shook her head as she tucked her hand into Sam's. Joey's life was his own. She would not try to influence him under any circumstances.

THE FIRST DAY they were in France, Sam and Maddie toured the vineyards. Martin and Vivi were delighted to see them. They gave them the royal treatment. Maddie began to feel guilty for their underlying, secret reason for being in France. She chatted with them over chilled wine, under an umbrella positioned in the valley, while Sam returned to the office, ostensibly to introduce himself to the employees. The truth was, he was going to examine some of the figures Jardin was inputting. He had also decided he would probably hire an auditor. There was a lot for him to do, and Maddie was nervous. It was difficult to keep a smile on her face when Martin and Vivi seemed so anxious to please her. If they were hiding something, she would never have known it.

She felt guilty until the second day, when Joey met her and Sam at a café for lunch. He brought his girlfriend, who was named Sasha.

Sasha didn't shave her underarms. Maddie swallowed, telling herself it was nothing unusual and that it wasn't up to her to do anything but like her brother's friend.

Sasha had a belly-button ring that glinted silver below the hem of her spaghetti-strap tank top. Maddie told herself it was fashionable, and so was the one in Sasha's tongue. She steeled herself and made herself eat the wonderfully prepared fish-and-pasta dish.

When Sasha lit a cigarette, Joey joined her. Maddie was shocked, because her brother was an avowed fitness nut. Sam grabbed her hand under the table, squeezing it, perhaps so she wouldn't say anything.

Maddie had no intention of saying a word. It was none of her business.

"I think college is so blasé," Sasha said. "I can't imagine what anyone can learn from stodgy, imagination-impaired professors that they can't learn in other, more stimulating ways." She pressed up against Joey's arm as she uttered this comment, her breasts straddling his large biceps.

Maddie swallowed. At that moment, something began moving up her leg. Her eyebrows raising, she realized it was Sasha's foot, inadvertently brushing her instead of Joey under the small table. Maddie gulped, sliding closer to Sam. Sasha realized her mistake, but instead of appearing shamefaced, merely gave her a daring smile.

Maddie wanted to pour pepper in the girl's hair, but Sam had her by the wrist now, reminding her to remain calm.

She was desperate to do so. "It was lovely to meet you," she said, gritting her teeth.

"We'll be sisters one day," Sasha told her. "Won't it be great?"

"Great," Maddie agreed.

"We can smoke a little—"

"Later," Joey interrupted.

"But I was going to invite your sister to—"

He dragged her off. Maddie heard him say grimly, "My sister doesn't even smoke cigarettes. She wouldn't touch weed or anything like that. And she's just had twins."

"I thought she seemed uptight," Sasha said, the words barely floating back.

Maddie whirled. "Has my brother lost his mind?"

Sam chuckled, taking her firmly by the arm. "Remember what you said. It's not your business. If she's what Joey wants—"

"But—"

"But nothing," Sam said firmly. "We're going to stick to our family. Our marriage. Our babies. What Joey wants is Joey's choice."

Maddie relaxed slightly as Sam put his arm around her. "I thought she'd be beautiful," she said piteously. "I wanted my baby brother to have the most wonderful woman in the world."

"I know," Sam told her. "Remember, we have a long history of this in our family."

Maddie shook her head. "She's not right for him!"

"It doesn't matter. It's his scholarship, his love life."

"I know you're right, but it makes me sad."

He turned her to him, kissing her until she was breathless. "Tell me again about your new goal."

"I'm concentrating on nothing but you," she said, her mind turning from Joey's gypsy girlfriend to Sam. "I'm in France, and alone with my husband."

She took a deep breath as the teasing kiss turned into something a great deal warmer. Hotter. "In fact, I view this as a second honeymoon. We needed a second honeymoon, Sam."

"You'd better believe it." He tugged her hand, pulling her quickly in the direction of a cab. "Second honeymoons call for special celebration."

They slid into a cab. Sam gave the address of his apartment, while he ran a searching hand up Maddie's leg. She put her head on his shoulder, barely able to wait until they reached their destination.

"I have something for you," he said when they got out. "It's special. We need to commemorate our honeymoon."

She could feel herself glowing with happiness. "I never thought I'd be here with you, so I don't really need anything to remember this time by. I'll never forget any of it."

"Still, I'd be remiss if I didn't at least attempt it."

They reached the stairs, hurrying up them. Sam opened the door, and they practically fell inside, rushing to be with each other.

Suddenly, they realized a voice was speaking.

"The answering machine," Sam said. "It's Martin." He jerked the phone off the receiver. "Hello?"

Maddie kicked off her heels. She glanced at Sam, whose face had turned serious. "I see," he said. "What course of action is open to us?"

After a few more moments of listening, Sam hung up. He closed his eyes for a second. Maddie's heart fell into her stomach. "What is it?"

"It appears that, bumbling as they may be, our parents were correct."

He sank into a chair. ''The Jardin books were being cooked, by Vivi's brother, Jean-Luc. He's just left the country with several million dollars of our money.''

Chapter Nineteen

It wasn't the money that worried Maddie. She was petrified Sam would have another attack of angina—only this one might escalate into a full-blown heart attack.

Her husband was a wreck. Facing financial ruin kept him on edge as he sorted through his options with Martin. His dream of owning his own company was gone. He became quiet and short-tempered with her.

She had to get back to her babies. The week was up and she couldn't leave them longer than that.

Yet she hated leaving Sam alone in France. He needed her, even if he didn't realize it. Even if he'd shut her out so completely she felt like there was a door between them.

Whatever magic had existed for the past weeks was gone like a puff of smoke.

When Sam put her on the plane for Texas, it was all she could do not to beg him to return with her. "Sam, I love you," she told him, her words desperate as she tried to bridge this new wall between them.

But he merely smiled sadly at her. "Take good care of the boys," he said.

The flight attendant ushered her into the plane. Sam waved once and then she couldn't see him anymore over the people who boarded after her.

It might take him months to recover the losses he'd suffered at Jardin. There was no way he could give in without losing a ton of money. People were counting on him to keep the company open.

He'd had a dream, and she wanted him to have what he'd worked so hard for. She forced the tears back, and the ones that wouldn't obey her she dried with a ragged tissue.

"Did you see Joey?" her mother asked when the family met her at the plane.

Maddie burst into tears, silently reaching for her babies.

The grandparents stared at each other, astounded. All she and Sam had told them was that he needed to stay in France for business.

"We were right, weren't we?" Severn asked.

She nodded at her father-in-law. "Vivi's brother."

"Thank heavens it wasn't Martin. I don't think Sam could have borne that," Franny said. "I don't like being right, but I sure am glad it wasn't Martin."

"I suppose that's the best way to look at it." Maddie shuddered and sniffled.

"It'll all turn out," her father said comfortingly. "Why, Sammy's got the world by the tail, hon. You just wait and see."

Maddie wasn't so sure. Sam had looked pretty broken to her, but maybe she'd just seen him through the mirror of her own pain. She knew how badly losing a dream could hurt the soul.

She would have given anything for Sam not to have suffered. And he was alone, something they had both vowed they wouldn't put up with again.

A strange tremor passed through her as she realized that once again they were separated, at a traumatic time when they should be standing side by side.

Whether on a dusty cotton farm or in loamy vineyards, people who loved each other should support each other. For better or worse.

But they weren't.

And he hadn't seemed to want to.

TIREDLY, Sam opened the door late one night after an unexpected shock. With some surprise, he gazed out at his brother-in-law. "Hey, Joey. Come on in."

Joey walked in, his beefy face somewhat sheepish.

"Where's Sasha?" Sam asked without thinking.

"That's what I want to talk to you about," Joey admitted, his blush deeper than some wine grapes Sam had seen.

He sighed inwardly, not wanting to have a love-lorn conversation with his brother-in-law. "All right," he said slowly. "Can I get you a beer?"

"No, thanks." Joey perched nervously on the edge of a leather sofa.

Sam tried not to think about the wonderful loving he and Maddie had shared on the sofa, and on the floor beside it. He missed her. But right now she didn't need to be around him while he was foul tempered and in dire straits with Jardin. Sometimes his panic was so strong he could taste it.

"Sasha's pregnant," Joey said.

Heat burst inside Sam's chest. It started out as a rosy flame, then licked into an intense inferno. He reached for a glass of milk and an antacid. "How can I help you?"

"I don't know," the brawny football player said. Then he burst into great, racking sobs. "All I could think to do was come to you. I always talk to Maddie about stuff. But I can't talk to her about this."

Sam frowned. "Why not?"

"Well, you know." Joey wiped at his face. "I don't want to upset her. I'm having a baby. She can't have any more. I just think it wouldn't be fair to involve Maddie in my problem. She's real sensitive about pregnancy."

Sam closed his eyes for a moment as he thought about Maddie. "I'm pretty sure your sister wouldn't be traumatized by this. She'd want to help you. Truthfully, it'd probably be better for you to talk to her about this than me."

Joey rubbed his palms over his jeans. "I've never been this scared."

"Having a baby is unsettling. Being a parent is overwhelming."

"I'm not ready," Joey said desperately.

Sam remembered that same attack of fear as if it had been yesterday. He hadn't believed he'd be a good father. When Joey had called him, his whole world had changed, like shifting colors in a kaleidoscope.

But he'd been so damn grateful for the miracle.

"Give yourself some time to get used to the idea," he said.

"I can't. Sasha wants to get married. I know that's the right thing to do," Joey said, his voice jagged with distress, "but I'm having second thoughts."

"I see." Sam leaned back in a recliner, realizing the ache in his chest was subsiding. "Sasha didn't exactly strike me as the conventional type."

"She's not. But she says money has a way of changing her mind about life's crass commercialism."

Sam cracked open a beer, focusing on Joey's babbling. "What money?"

"I'm not exactly sure. Mine, I guess."

"I wasn't aware you had any," Sam said carefully.

"I don't, really. Maybe she meant my football scholarship."

"But she doesn't approve of college."

Joey scratched his head. "I guess after college there might be pro football. If I got picked up in the draft."

"Seems like there's something missing in your relationship, Joey. Like there's a major miscommunication."

"I know." Joey put his head in his hands. "I don't think Maddie liked Sasha, and that's when I decided I was just dating her to defy Mom and Dad. It was fun at first, because Sasha's out of the ordinary, and our family has always been pretty regular. Mom and Dad can make you crazy with their nosiness, but other than that, they're definitely not Mr. and Mrs. Excitement."

"And Sasha is?"

"Definitely. But then, I could tell Maddie was practically tying her tongue in knots to keep from giving me a scolding, and I started cooling off on Sasha. Maddie doesn't stick her two cents in unless she has to. She's always tried real hard to leave that family gene behind."

"I believe she mentioned that to me."

Joey nodded. "I told Sasha I wanted to slow down a little bit, especially since I was going to have to report for training soon. But she said she was pregnant. And then I didn't know what to think."

I think you got set up, Sam wanted to say. Why, he didn't know.

He had just as much faith in Maddie as Joey did, though. She would be a great one to talk to about everything. Glancing toward the phone, Sam told himself to call her. To tell her to come back.

But he really wasn't much fun these days—and he and Maddie needed fun. Romance.

With the missing money, and now Joey, Sam didn't think he had enough energy left to kick-start his marriage with the romance they needed.

MADDIE ADVANCED upon the flowing water statue in her bathroom with a determined gleam in her eye. In her hand, she carried assorted tools. "You, sister," she told the statue, "are in for a bit of adjustment under your skirt."

The statue spit water in reply. Maddie laid her tools on the bathroom counter. "The truth is, I used to enjoy your little tic. Maybe I even related to it. Not anymore. When I get through with you, you're either going to be a whole statue or you're going back in your box for a ride to the store."

It took her an hour but Maddie finally located the various valves and tubes. Following the directions on the box, she made some adjustments.

When she was finished, she stood the silent statue upright. "You will flow and not spray. You will pour peacefully and tranquilly and be a vision of the womanhood you were meant to portray. If you spit, you go back. You are a statue, not a real woman, and I do not have to love your imperfection. I may have learned to love myself, flaws and all, but yours were priced at $45.99. That's cash I may need, come to think of it, so mind your manners and be fabulously feminine."

She plugged in the statue, and peaceful streams of water swirled from the appropriate jet into the bowl.

Maddie sighed with relief as the woman proudly achieved her mission of water collection. She really was beautiful, now that all her wires were uncrossed.

"Maddie?" Franny called into the master bathroom.

"In here."

"Are you decent?" her mother asked.

Maddie smiled. "Come on in. I was just doing something I should have done a long time ago."

Franny came into the room, the cordless phone in her hand. "Oh, doesn't she look regal! I always knew the plumbing would work just fine one day." She grinned at Maddie, proud of her daughter's handiwork. "Sam's on the phone."

She gestured with the phone at Maddie, who eagerly took it and shooed her mother from the bathroom. "Hi, Sam."

"How's my wife?"

His voice sounded a bit disconnected over the wires. "She misses you dreadfully."

"I miss you, too."

"How's everything in France?" She dipped a finger in the water, which ran cool and smooth into the basin as she waited for Sam's answer.

"Vivi's just about talked Jean-Luc into giving himself up."

"Oh, how heartbreaking for her. I would die if Joey was in trouble like that! I'd have to thrash him, and then lecture him, and he would never, ever go near trouble again. I'm positive Vivi's too ladylike for that, though."

Sam cleared his throat. "Actually, she's pretty volatile when she gets upset. She has quite a temper on her, which has been a revelation for easygoing Martin. The fact that her brother couldn't deal with the family business being sold apparently has no bearing on her. She's all but told her brother that if he doesn't bring back the money and honor the spirit of the deal worked out between them and me…" He halted for a moment. "Never mind. The rest of it wasn't pretty."

"Oh, dear. I'm sorry, Sam."

"It's not as bad as it could be. Apparently when our folks were over here, poking around and generally being 'American', as Vivi politely termed it—"

"Brash and unforgivably nosy," Maddie said with a smile.

"Exactly, but she's too refined to say that. Anyway, they apparently spooked Jean-Luc. He realized his game could be up at any moment, and skipped with the money.''

"I guess we have to thank the folks, this time, for their meddling.'' She laughed, noticing instantly that Sam didn't. "How's everything else, Sam? You sound so tired.''

"I'm not tired. I didn't call about Jardin, though. I have something to tell you, which I shouldn't, but I'm going to risk some old-fashioned nosiness myself.''

"Oh, my. I am intrigued.''

He cleared his throat. "Now, I don't want you thrashing Joey, honey. This is important. He doesn't want to talk to you about this. Well, he does and he doesn't. He's afraid to hurt your feelings, but... Sasha's pregnant.''

Ten thoughts flew into Maddie's brain at once, none of which came out coherent. "I wonder if her belly-button ring will have to come out?''

"Maddie—''

"That's a shame because they're awfully young, but I know my grandparents said the same thing about my parents, so maybe passion flows in our genes at a young age. Still, it's none of—''

"Maddie!''

"Yes, Sam?''

"This is your business. You are allowed to stick your nose in. Joey wants you to, but he's too afraid to call you.''

"Afraid? Why? I wouldn't thrash him over a pregnancy. I haven't been able to beat up on him since he entered junior high, technically.''

"No, but he's always listened to his big sister. You're up on some kind of sibling pedestal that he strains to live up to."

"Then why is he afraid to call me?"

"He's afraid you'll be upset that he's having a child and you...can't."

She stared at the beautiful statue gracing the bathroom, the water streaming in a feminine, earth mother way. "No," she said softly, "I'm over all that. My children and my husband are all that matter to me, besides our families. My man and my babies make me whole."

"I love you," Sam said, his voice distant over the long-distance line. "I miss you and my sons."

"I love you, too," she said, her heart yearning for something completely different right now. "Sam, you tell Joey his big sister loves him, too."

"I will. Maddie, I miss you."

She smiled to herself. He wouldn't much longer. There was a new mission in her life, and it was one she wanted with all her heart.

Chapter Twenty

Sam sat up, astonished when he heard a key grating in the lock.

He was even more stunned a second later when Maddie breezed in, carting two baby carriers.

"Maddie!" Jumping to his feet, he hurried over to hug her and help her inside.

"Meter's running, Sam," she said with a joyful laugh. "If we've lost everything, you'd better hurry down and rescue my bags from the cab driver. He needs to be paid, and I didn't stop to get enough francs."

Sam hurried to pay the cab driver, his heart soaring. He was back as fast as he could to soundly kiss his wife and then his two babies. "They've grown so much! You boys are so big you look like your uncle Joey! I've missed you!" He kissed Maddie again. "I can't believe you flew all that way with two babies by yourself."

"Neither could our mothers. They approved of me joining you, but they were terrified of recirculated air in the airplane. And germs in the airport. If they'd had their way, they would have piped the babies under the ocean in a tube, I think.''

Sam laughed, freeing first Henry, then Hayden from the carriers. ''If my mother had warned me you were coming, I would have run the sweeper around the apartment.''

Maddie kicked off her shoes, giving him a sexy-siren smile. ''That's not what I would have wanted you to do.''

''You're right. I would have procured some fabulous French wine, maybe some roses.'' He went to sit beside her, so they could be together as they held their children. ''I wouldn't have been able to sleep, I would have been so excited.''

''You needed your rest. These little guys sleep through the night now, but they sure know how to keep people running during the day.'' Maddie smiled at Sam, her head tilted just enough so that he could see the pretty green of her eyes in the dim apartment light.

''You're beautiful,'' he told her. ''Somehow, you look different.''

''I feel different.''

''What made you decide to come back?''

''I needed you. And you sounded tired, troubled. Two sets of shoulders carry the burden much better than one, Sam. I want us to share the good times and the bad. It's what we've never really done before, and I know we can now. I've put the tears away for good. No more waterworks and regret for me.''

''You didn't come all this way just to bawl out your brother? He should be here in about five minutes.''

"Why?" Maddie asked, bouncing Henry gently as she looked at Sam.

"He and Sasha are getting married this afternoon. He didn't call you?"

Silently, she shook her head. Sam could see that she was confused.

"That's not the real reason you're here?"

"I've told you why I'm here. It's because of the good times and the bad. It's because we're going to grow together in this marriage, and even when everything we try to build burns down around our ears, we're going to help each other find the new growth just beneath the charred surface."

"I'm glad you feel that way. I've been so turned in on myself, Maddie. All I could think of was how disappointed you must be in my inability to provide for you."

"What?" Outrage made her voice a yelp. "Sam Winston, how could you think such a thing?"

"Probably the same way you worry about giving me more children. I'm fine with these two. I always was. In fact, I was fine with none, except that I blamed myself for not being able to get you pregnant then."

"That doesn't matter anymore." Maddie smiled at him, her gaze warm. "And Sam, please don't ever think I need to be provided for. We will take care of this family, you and I. Together."

She sat back down again, hugging him close. He put his arm around her shoulders. "Does this mean I can give you what I tried to give you a few weeks ago on our second honeymoon?"

Banging on the door halted her answer. Maddie

stared at Sam, her eyes huge in her face. She might not want to get involved in her brother's affairs, but he could tell it was eating at her something fierce. Reluctantly, he got up to open the door.

"Maddie!" Joey cried when he saw his sister and his nephews.

She jumped up, rushing to hug her brother. He enveloped her in a bear hug, careful of the baby she held in her arms.

"Did Sam call you?" Joey asked.

"No. I came to be with my husband. He just told me where you're going this afternoon." For the first time, she realized Sam had on a dark suit, much like the one her brother wore. She'd thought he was dressed for work. "You're dressed for a wedding," she said to Sam.

"I'm best man," he told her, his expression slightly worried.

"Sam Winston! You weren't going to tell me!" Maddie put a hand on her hip as she cradled the baby to her chest with the other. "You let me pour my heart out to you, and you were holding back!"

"I told you the who and the why. I just couldn't tell you the when, Maddie. Don't be upset. I knew if you found out the wedding was imminent, you'd be over here in a flash. I thought it was better for you to be in Texas, where you have our families to help you."

She blinked, her breath knocked right out of her. "I don't believe it."

"Don't be angry," Joey begged. "I didn't want anyone to know. In time, I'll tell the folks, but right now, I just can't. They're going to be heartbroken."

"Yes, they will be," Maddie said softly. "It certainly feels as though mine is breaking. I told myself I wasn't going to do this, but doggone it, I am, anyway. It may be coming a little late, and I hate to rain on your happiness, but…" She took a deep breath, glancing at the men who stared at her warily. "Marriage gets rocky, Joey. If this woman isn't the dream partner you've always envisioned, don't go to the church today."

"Actually, we're not getting married in a church," Joey said, his face pink. "She wanted a New Age ceremony."

"That's fine," Maddie said, "if it's what you both agreed on."

He didn't answer.

"And babies are demanding. You're both prepared to give up major chunks of your lives to dedicate to this infant?"

"I know I am. I'm not totally irresponsible."

"Just in the matter of birth control," she reminded him, keeping her tone gentle.

"I was certain I wasn't irresponsible," Joey assured her. "I've heard that lecture so many times over the years from Mom and Dad it's seared into my head! I…used protection every time. Sasha says sometimes these things just happen."

Maddie's gaze flew to Sam's. His eyes were as worried as she knew hers must be. She knew her brother so well—there was more going on than he was telling her. "Joey," she said quietly, "are you upset about not going back to college?"

His lips twisted into an uneven line. "I didn't

make that swift of grades last quarter, Maddie. I can't play the fall season. I got suspended.''

"Oh, boy." Her knees gave way, and she dropped onto the sofa. She stared up at him. "Why didn't you tell me?"

"You were busy with your own problems. It seemed selfish to bother you."

She shook her head. "It seems I was the one being selfish. I should have been there for you to talk to."

"Neither of you were being selfish," Sam said. "These are the hard moments families face together. Joey should have been studying harder, and we should have been paying more attention to our marriage so he wouldn't worry about coming to you when he needed advice."

"I have a little late-breaking advice, Joey, now that I'm paying attention," Maddie said softly. "You don't have to marry Sasha just because you're afraid to let Mom and Dad down. They'll get over it. Yes, they'll be disappointed, but they're tough."

Sam came to sit next to her, putting his hand over hers, and Maddie felt the connection, the fusing of their lives. "Trust me, when you've found love, it'll be the most wonderful moment of your life," she told Joey, her heart singing from being able to give him good counsel on something she knew about first-hand. "I want you to be happy. Our parents would want you to be happy."

"How do I tell her?" Joey asked.

Sam and Maddie looked at each other.

"Just meet her and tell her the truth. I think per-haps you should talk to her about establishing paternity, so that Martin can work up some legal documents where the child is concerned.''

"Establish paternity?'' Joey sank into a nearby chair. "To make sure I'm the father?''

"Joey,'' Maddie protested, her tone kind. "We're not trying to be hard on you, but we don't really know this woman. All Sam and I are saying is that it would be best to have this sort of test done. That will give you some more time to think about getting married.''

"She's not going to like that idea,'' Joey said, scratching his head. "She's always talking about how cool it will be to be part of the Jardin scene. Jardin is a big deal in France.''

"How does Jardin fit into her scene?'' Maddie asked, beginning to see where this was going but wanting to hear it confirmed.

"It's a famous company. Vivi and Jean-Luc are very generous, glamorous people in France. I guess Sasha thought marrying me would give her access to some of that.''

"And Sasha thinks life is going to be fast boats and Lear jets.'' She grinned at Sam. "Sasha's welcome to our debt, if she really wants to be part of Jardin. In fact, why don't you mention that to her?''

"Mention what?'' Joey's face was utterly blank.

"You didn't tell him, did you?'' Maddie asked Sam.

"No. He had plenty on his mind as it was.''

Maddie started to laugh. "Tell him, Sam.''

Sam said ruefully, "Jardin was embezzled by Jean-Luc. We're trying to recover millions of dollars right now. It could take years, Joey. Truthfully, there isn't any money for anything faster than a rusty tug-boat or a paper airplane.''

Then he chuckled. This made the babies start a little as they lay in their parents' arms, but they didn't cry out. Maddie thought they were already readjusting to being around their father, which made her proud. She grinned at her brother. "Sam and I are going to rebuild Jardin together, from the dirt up if we have to, into the successful wine company he's—we've—always dreamed of. If Sasha wants in on the ground floor, you can tell her we have some openings for farm workers and bottlers.''

It seemed like a burden lifted from Joey's shoulders. "She likes a more glamorous life. I don't think that's an offer she'll take me up on.''

Maddie and Sam shared a smile. "We don't think you'll regret it,'' she said. "When the right person comes along, there won't be a doubt in your mind you're doing the right thing.''

THREE HOURS LATER, Joey called with good news. "You were right. Sasha decided marriage wasn't for her once I told her about the embezzling problem. Funny thing was, it was on the front page of today's newspaper. She was reading it as I caught up to her in the park.''

"Joey, I'm so sorry,'' Maddie said.

"I'm not. She acted like I had an advanced case of rabies. The most amazing thing was, when I asked her what we were going to do about the baby, she said she'd started her, um—''

"Never mind. I know where you're going.'' Maddie interrupted with a grin. There were some subjects even the closest of brothers and sisters didn't have to discuss.

"The all-clear happened this afternoon, Sasha told me," Joey said in a rush.

"Imagine that." Maddie rolled her eyes. *Right after she read the paper,* she thought, but she didn't say it out loud. Babies were a special blessing for people who wanted them; it made her angry that the weapon of fatherhood had been used against her trusting brother.

"I'm going back to school," Joey said cheerfully. "In fact, I'm calling from the airport. I've got a flight out today. As soon as I land, I'm going to tell the folks about my grades, and that I'm going to work double hard to make it up. I'll worry about football later. Maybe I'll play, maybe I won't, but I definitely want to clear my conscience with them."

"I'm so proud of you. Although you should be prepared, Joey. You know they'll probably switch the full depth of their helpfulness from me to you. I'm out of their reach in France."

"That's okay," Joey said, and she could hear the grin in his voice. "I need their guidance more than you do."

"I have Sam to keep me level."

Sam patted her leg, supporting her as he listened to the conversation.

"Thanks, Maddie," Joey said. "For everything."

She smiled. "No problem. It's what sisters are for. Remember, I'm just a phone call away. Well, what am I saying? You know very well how to call France."

They laughed together at the gentle reminder of

Joey's phone call to Sam when his twins were born. "I never talked to you about that," she reminded him.

"Go ahead. Chew my ears off. I deserve it for meddling."

Maddie's face shone with happiness. "Thank you," she said. "Thank you for helping Sam and me get back together."

"Anytime," Joey said. "That's what brothers are for."

WHEN THE BABIES went to sleep that evening, Sam hurried his wife toward the bed. "I'm heartily sick of sleeping alone. I've missed you," he told her. "I thought I would go mad staring up at this ceiling in the darkness. We've had too many months apart. Your body was made to fit next to mine, so I hope you're planning on staying a long time."

She motioned for him to turn around. He did so, and she quickly changed into a short, sexy-as-sin red nightie. "Husband," she cooed, "you can turn around now. I have something to make you feel better—"

He fairly leaped across the bed to drag her onto it with him. She shrieked, but only for effect. "I missed you, too," she said, cozying up to him.

He fingered the short length of her nightie appreciatively. "Nice of you to bring me such a present from the States. I'm positive we're about to get reacquainted quickly. And very intimately." His eyes turned sober. "Maddie, I really am glad as heck you're here. And you have perfect timing. Five minutes later, and who knows where we'd all have been.''

She gave him a knowing smile. "I think I'd still be in your bed. Somehow. I was determined not to be put out again."

"I never put you out."

"You became very grumpy and convinced you didn't want me in France.

"It doesn't matter," he said with a growl, burying his face between her lace-edged breasts. "From now on, all our trials and tribulations are a joint effort."

"And the good times, and the happiness. It's what we promised. It's what we should have been doing all along."

"Nothing like a second chance to make something stick for good, I always say." He reached into the nightstand and pulled out a velvet box. "Now, Maddie, I've been trying to talk to you about this for several weeks. This is something I give to you, in honor of our—"

"I know. Our second time."

"Right." He grinned, flipping open the box to reveal the diamond set he'd given her at their wedding.

"You bought them back," she breathed.

"Well, yes. They hold a lot of happy memories."

She smiled at him. "Thank you so much, Sam. I promise not to ever sell them again."

"You'll have to keep that promise, woman. I made one little change to them."

He turned the rings over, so that she could see an inscription had been written on the inside of the wedding band.

"'Surprise! Surprise!'" Maddie read, "'I love you. Sam.'"

She looked up, her eyes full of joyous tears. "That's no surprise at all," she said. "I didn't need for you to write it twice."

"Well, that," he said, sliding the rings back on her finger, "is to express my joy at fathering twins. I wanted it written twice, so each baby would be celebrated."

"Surprise, surprise," she murmured as she slid her arms around Sam's neck, bringing her face close to his. "I love you, too."

He kissed her once, and then he kissed her again—just in case there was any doubt left in her mind that the second time was going to be everything they'd ever wanted.

There wasn't any doubt left for either of them. Five seconds later the red-hot nightie lay on the floor, as Sam and Maddie discovered the joys of holy matrimony all over again.

Epilogue

France, seven months later

"Sam!" Maddie tore through the foyer of the flat, instantly catching the attention of the toddlers and her husband as he was enjoying a morning of chasing his children. She flew to him, nearly catapulting into his outstretched arms, then locking her legs around his waist. "I'm pregnant!" she shrieked. "We're going to have another baby!"

"A baby!" The floor seemed to rock under Sam's feet. "Are you sure?"

"Yes, I'm sure! I've just been to the clinic." She kissed her husband, expressing all the joy racing through her. "It's an unexpected miracle! Abby told me several months ago that sometimes it's easier to get pregnant the second time, like turning on a tap. Goodness knows we've been busily testing her theory, but I never dreamed it would happen!"

They smiled at each other, dazed, stunned and profoundly grateful. Sam hugged her, before sitting down with her in his lap. The toddlers made their way over, hanging on to whatever assisted their trembling steps. Maddie swept them both up into her lap. "What a surprise. What a shock!" She threw back her head and laughed. Sam chuckled with her, and the babies smiled because they could hear their parents' joy.

"It's going to be wonderful to go through this pregnancy together," Sam said. He put his arms around his family and held them to him. He smiled and put his chin on Maddie's shoulder.

She turned her face to his so that their foreheads touched, and whispered, "I love you," at the very same time he said, "I love you, Maddie."

Their soft laughter mingled as they enjoyed the melding of their thoughts. And then they said the words a second time, celebrating this new miracle—together.

Here's a sneak peek
at Tina Leonard's Intrigue,

A MAN OF HONOR,

coming next month
from Harlequin.

Prologue

The north Texas night was colder than most, stinging Cord Greer's face as he went out into the February storm to get firewood. Wind-driven sleet slashed across his cheeks, but he merely lowered his Stetson and tried to ignore the chilling sensation that had been bugging him for the past two hours.

Something was wrong. He could feel it as sure as the ice storm gripping Crookseye Canyon. What really had his skin creeping was that he'd had this feeling only once before, when his brother, Hunt, had been in a car crash. It was as if Cord had felt the impact himself that night. Hunt had walked away from the crash, but Cord could still remember the peculiar sensation that he'd been right there in the car with his brother.

Tonight he'd felt a different kind of impact. This one closed over him with dark fingers of dread as his soul felt a rending, a tearing of one half from the other.

He shook it off, telling himself the storm—and too much time alone on his ranch—were making him imagine things. Being half-Navajo didn't necessarily make him a mind-reader, as some people seemed to think. But he did feel deeply, a trait he'd developed at a point in his life he couldn't even remember.

Taking an armload of firewood inside, he tried to force his mind off of Hunt's latest secret assignment.

The knock at his front door ten minutes later came as no surprise. Though he'd been dozing in the recliner in front of a crackling fire, part of him had been waiting. He got up reluctantly, bracing himself for what he knew he would hear.

Opening the door, he stared at the two men standing in the bitter, black night. Framed by the yellow light from the porch lantern, they looked serious and official.

"Mr. Greer?" one asked, flashing some type of identification, which Cord ignored. He kept his gaze fastened on the men instead, nodding once.

"We regret to inform you that your brother was killed tonight while on a sensitive assignment. Though we can't divulge more than that at the present time, you may rest assured that your brother, Hunt Greer, died an honorable death."

The fools. Who did they think they were kidding? Hunt wasn't dead. Cord had felt something strange, an odd sensation passing through his soul, but not the disconnection he would feel if Hunt was dead. He waited, his jaw tight.

His silence appeared to unnerve the smaller officer. "We would have informed his fiancée." He checked his paper. "Tessa should be notified. Regretfully, we don't know her location."

You never will, Cord vowed. He wouldn't allow these two lame excuses to go to Tessa's door and frighten her out of her wits with their lack of emotion. *Regret to inform you.* She was carrying Hunt's child, and the shock these unfeeling clods would give her could cause her and the baby harm.

"I'm sorry," he said with a shrug. "I'm not aware of her location myself." He told the lie easily to spare her the pain.

The men shifted. "You don't know where your brother's fiancée is?" the taller man asked, his voice edged with surprised disbelief—and obvious disappointment.

Cord noted the foreign accent, not quite Mexican. Spanish more likely. That put him on his guard even more. "No, I don't," he said softly, his voice as clear and hard as the ice forming on the roads. "My brother and I weren't close."

He shut the door. He knew Tessa was at the usual spot she and Hunt rendezvoused after he completed his latest assignment. Cord had pleaded with his brother not to take his fiancée to places that teemed with unrest, pointing out that he risked her life as well as his. Should some subversive foreign faction ever figure out Hunt was breaking their codes and moving equipment and people in and out of high-risk positions, he would be in great danger. Tessa might even divert his attention, getting both of them killed.

Nonsense, Hunt had retorted with a laugh. Tessa and Hunt were two people who lived life to the fullest, while Cord stayed on his farm, watching after his cattle and tending a few crops. Hunt was an adventurer, and Tessa had caught his fever. *Having her with me sharpens my focus,* he'd told Cord. *I'm knife-edge aware when I've got her with me. She makes every moment that much more defined.*

Cord had turned away, but not in disgust at his brother's selfishness. He'd completely understood. Tessa was the kind of woman any man would want to protect, and to give his heart and soul to.

She'd stolen Hunt's entire being the first time he'd met her—and then she'd stolen Cord's.

Coming in June from

HARLEQUIN®

AMERICAN ◆ ROMANCE®

MAITLAND MATERNITY

When two sets
of twins are born at
Maitland Maternity Hospital on
the same day, unforgettable surprises
are sure to follow. Don't miss the fun, the
romance, the joy...as two special couples find
love just outside the delivery room door.

Watch for:
SURPRISE! SURPRISE!
by Tina Leonard
On sale June 2000.

I DO! I DO!
by Jacqueline Diamond
On sale July 2000.

And there will be many more Maitland Maternity
stories when a special twelve-book continuity series
launches in August 2000.

Don't miss any of these stories by wonderful
authors such as Marie Ferrarella, Jule McBride,
Muriel Jensen and Judy Christenberry.

Available at your favorite retail outlet.

HARLEQUIN®
Makes any time special ™

Visit us at www.eHarlequin.com.

HARMMDD

HARLEQUIN®
SUPERROMANCE®

You are now entering

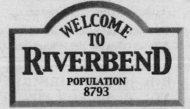

WELCOME TO
RIVERBEND
POPULATION
8793

Riverbend...the kind of place where everyone knows
your name—and your business. Riverbend...home of
the River Rats—a group of small-town sons and
daughters who've been friends since high school.

The Rats are all grown up now. Living their lives and
learning that some days are good and some days
aren't—and that you can get through anything
as long as you have your friends.

Starting in July 2000, Harlequin Superromance brings
you Riverbend—six books about the River Rats and
the Midwest town they live in.

BIRTHRIGHT by **Judith Arnold** (July 2000)
THAT SUMMER THING by **Pamela Bauer** (August 2000)
HOMECOMING by **Laura Abbot** (September 2000)
LAST-MINUTE MARRIAGE by **Marisa Carroll** (October 2000)
A CHRISTMAS LEGACY by **Kathryn Shay** (November 2000)

Available wherever Harlequin books are sold.

HARLEQUIN®
Makes any time special ™

Visit us at www.eHarlequin.com   HSRIVER

HARLEQUIN®
AMERICAN ◆ ROMANCE®

WANTS TO SEND YOU HOME FOR THE HOLIDAYS!

Just write in and tell us in 250 words or less
why you'd like to go home for the holidays.

Take your pick of holidays...
Thanksgiving or Christmas!

Our judging panel will select
2 lucky Grand Prize winners

The Grand Prize:
ROUND-TRIP AIRFARE
TO TAKE YOU HOME FOR THE HOLIDAYS
via American Airlines

5 First Prize Winners will receive:
$100 in long distance gift certificates.

DON'T MISS YOUR CHANCE TO WIN!
ENTER NOW! No Purchase Necessary.
Contest ends July 31, 2000.

HARLEQUIN®
Makes any time special ™

AmericanAirlines®

Home For The Holidays Contest 9119

Attach your name, address and phone number to your entry telling us why you want to go
"Home For The Holidays" and mail your entry via first-class mail to "Harlequin Home For
The Holidays Contest 9119": In the U.S.: P.O. Box 9069, Buffalo, NY 14269-9069; In
Canada: P.O. Box 637, Fort Erie, Ontario, L2A 5X3. Or enter on-line at
www.eHarlequin.com/homefortheholidays.

**Essays will be judged by a panel of members of the Harlequin editorial and marketing
staff based on the following criteria:**

- Sincerity — 40%
- Originality and Creativity — 35%
- Emotionally Compelling — 25%

No purchase necessary—Purchase or acceptance of a product offer does not improve your
chances of winning. Contest open to residents of U.S. (except Puerto Rico) and Canada who
are 18 years of age or older. Void where prohibited by law. Contest ends July 31, 2000.

For complete official contest rules and entry form send a self-addressed stamped envelope
(residents of Washington or Vermont may omit return postage) to "Harlequin Home for
the Holidays Contest 9119 Rules" (in the U.S.) P.O. Box 9069, Buffalo, NY 14269-9069;
(in Canada) P.O. Box 637, Fort Erie, ON, Canada L2A 5X3.

HARHFTH3

HARLEQUIN HOME FOR THE HOLIDAYS CONTEST 9119
OFFICIAL RULES
NO PURCHASE NECESSARY TO ENTER

1. To enter, follow directions published in the offer to which you are responding. Contest begins April 1, 2000 and ends on July 31, 2000. Method of entry may vary. Mailed entries must be postmarked by July 31, 2000 and received by August 7, 2000.

2. Contest entry may be, at times, presented via the Internet but will be restricted solely to residents of certain geographic areas that are disclosed on the Web site. To enter via the Internet, if permissible, access the Harlequin romance Web site (http://www.eHarlequin.com) and follow the directions displayed online. Online entries must be received by 11:59 p.m. E.S.T on July 31, 2000.

   In lieu of submitting an entry online, enter by mail by hand-printing (or typing) on an 8 " x 11" plain piece of paper, your name, address (including zip code), contest number/name, and in 250 words or fewer, tell us why you would like to go home for the Thanksgiving or Christmas holiday. Mail via first-class mail to: Harlequin Home for the Holidays Contest 9119, (in the U.S.) P.O. Box 9069, Buffalo, NY 14269-9069, (in Canada) P.O. Box 637, Fort Erie, Ontario, Canada L2A 5X3.

   Limit one entry per person, household address and e-mail address. Online and/or mailed entries received from persons residing in geographic areas in which Internet entry is not permissible will be disqualified.

3. Essays will be judged by a panel of members of the Harlequin editorial and marketing staff based on the following criteria:

   Sincerity—40%

   Originality and Creativity—35%

   Emotionally Compelling—25%

   In the event of a tie, duplicate prizes will be awarded. Decisions of the judges are final.

4. All entries become the property of Torstar Corp. and will not be returned. No responsibility is assumed for lost, late, illegible, incomplete, inaccurate, nondelivered or misdirected mail or misdirected e-mail, for technical, hardware or software failures of any kind, lost or unavailable network connections, or failed, incomplete, garbled or delayed computer transmission or any human error that may occur in the receipt or processing of the entries in this contest.

5. Contest open only to residents of the U.S. (except Puerto Rico) and Canada, who are 18 years of age or older, and is void wherever prohibited by law; all applicable laws and regulations apply. Any litigation within the Province of Québec respecting the conduct or organization of a publicity contest may be submitted to the Régie des alcools, des courses et des jeux for a ruling. Any litigation respecting the awarding of a prize may be submitted to the Régie des alcools, des courses et des jeux only for the purpose of helping the parties reach a settlement. Employees and immediate family members of Torstar Corp. and D.L. Blair, Inc., their affiliates, subsidiaries and all other agencies, entities and persons connected with the use, marketing or conduct of this contest are not eligible to enter. Taxes on prizes are the sole responsibility of winners. Acceptance of any prize offered constitutes permission to use winner's name, photograph or other likeness for the purposes of advertising, trade and promotion on behalf of Torstar Corp., its affiliates and subsidiaries without further compensation to the winner, unless prohibited by law.

6. Winners will be determined no later than August 31, 2000, and will be notified by mail. Winners will be required to sign and return an Affidavit of Eligibility form within 15 days after winner notification. Noncompliance within that time period may result in disqualification and an alternate winner may be selected. Winners of trip must execute a Release of Liability prior to ticketing and must possess required travel documents (e.g. passport, photo ID) where applicable. Trip must be taken on dates specified by sponsor. No substitution of prize permitted by winner. Torstar Corp. and D.L. Blair, Inc., their parents, affiliates and subsidiaries are not responsible for errors in printing or electronic presentation of contest, entries and/or game pieces. In the event of printing or other errors, which may result in unintended prize values or duplication of prizes, all affected game pieces or entries shall be null and void. If for any reason the Internet portion of the contest is not capable of running as planned, including infection by computer virus, bugs, tampering, unauthorized intervention, fraud, technical failures or any other causes beyond the control of Torstar Corp. which corrupt or affect the administration, secrecy, fairness, integrity or proper conduct of the contest, Torstar Corp. reserves the right, at its sole discretion, to disqualify any individual who tampers with the entry process and to cancel, terminate, modify or suspend the contest or the Internet portion thereof. In the event of a dispute regarding an online entry, the entry will be deemed submitted by the authorized holder of the e-mail account submitted at the time of entry. Authorized account holder is defined as the natural person who is assigned to an e-mail address by an Internet access provider, online service provider or other organization that is responsible for arranging e-mail address for the domain associated with the submitted e-mail address. Purchase or acceptance of a product offer does not improve your chances of winning.

7. Prizes: (2) Two Grand Prizes—(1) One ticket for round-trip coach air transportation to winner's choice destination to go home for either this Thanksgiving or Christmas holiday from gateway airport nearest winner's home, including round-trip ground transportation to/from airport (approximate value: $3,500 ea.); (5) Five First Prizes—$100 long distance gift certificates. Limit one prize per person. All prizes are valued in U.S. currency.

8. For a list of winners (available after September 29, 2000), send a self-addressed, stamped envelope to: Harlequin Home for the Holidays Contest 9119 Winners, P.O. Box 4200 Blair, NE 68009-4200.

Contest sponsored by Torstar Corp., P.O. Box 9042, Buffalo, NY 14269-9042.

HARRULES